RUNNING BLIND

Gwen Hernandez

RUNNING BLIND

ISBN: 978-1983688805

This book is a work of fiction. Names, characters, places, and incidents are the product of the author's imagination or are used fictitiously. Any resemblance to actual events, locales, or persons, living or dead, is coincidental.

First edition: January 2018

Cover design by Kim Killion.

This book was written and formatted in Scrivener.

www.gwenhernandez.com

For my grandmother, Lillian, quiet renegade, dedicated nurse, crossword maven, and remarkable woman of rare smiles who faced late-life amputation with grace.

ACKNOWLEDGMENTS

Writing a book is never a solitary endeavor. First, I have to thank my husband and college boys, who were incredibly understanding as I worked on revisions during our stay in a temporary beach house while house hunting just several days before Christmas. Thank you for the dinners, dishes, dog walks, and sunsets.

Also, to awesome author and good friend, Rachel Grant, whose keen insights—as always—helped me sort out some key issues in the book. Thanks for the notes and the cheerleading!

Writing this book wouldn't have been as much fun without Ellie Ashe and Lily Danes forcing me to leave the house every now and then. I'm going to miss you, ladies!

Thanks to my Kiss & Thrill sisters, for having a ready cheer or virtual hug as needed. XOXOXO

Gwen Hayes and Sonnet Fitzgerald helped me make this story stronger, and Kim Killion conjured up another awesome cover. You ladies rock.

Tessa Murphy, I finally got your name in a book. Enjoy!

Tremendous thanks to prosthetist Dave Scurti, who was generous with his time and expertise. He helped me immeasurably with the technical details on Kurt's legs and capabilities. Any mistakes are definitely my own.

Finally, thank you readers for your enthusiasm for Kurt and Caitlyn's story. I'm sorry this one took so long, and I hope I did it justice. You're the number one reason I write, and I appreciate you.

CHAPTER ONE

SOMETHING WAS OFF. THE CARIBBEAN jungle beyond the chain-link fence had gone quiet.

The back of Caitlyn's neck prickled and beads of moisture gathered on her skin as she and her dog strolled the grassy strip at the edge of the runway. Nascent sunlight washed the sky in pale gold, banishing the shadows, and at the end of his leash, Rockley lifted his leg and peed on a fencepost.

If something were wrong, wouldn't he sense it too?

"Come on, Ro." She flicked the leash and he quit sniffing the ground.

No less than eight guards tracked her progress toward the plane. Their presence should have made her feel secure.

About halfway to her ugly-but-reliable six-seater prop, Treavor Lambert and three men entered the airfield through a small gate that led to the house. His two guards—Jack, a hulking white man with a shaved head and a thick beard, and a lanky black man with cornrows named Christophe—flanked him. With their AK-47s and shiny muscles, the pair could have walked straight out of *Soldier of Fortune* magazine.

His son Glenn came third. *Damn.* He was back from his three-week tour of Europe. Late twenties, sandy hair, blue eyes, chiseled features, gym-honed muscles, and a tennis-court tan. The type who looked airbrushed and superfluous despite his Ivy League education. The type who probably tortured kittens and charmed his mother with the same zeal.

"Good morning, Ms. Brevard," Lambert said in his deep, booming voice.

She stopped and waited for the group to join her. "Morning."

Lambert somehow looked cool and fresh in a gray suit tailored for his tall, trim frame, not a single strand of salt-and-pepper hair out of place. He bent over and stroked Rockley's black fur. "He looks better every week. You're taking good care of him."

"Thank you, sir. He just needed a little love." Someone had dumped the lab mix on the road near Rockley Beach, beaten and bloody, his coat matted and mud-caked. The poor boy was only now starting to look healthy again. "Lucky he's a good flier or I wouldn't have been able to keep him."

As if she could have abandoned him to who-knows-what fate.

"Dad," Glenn said, stepping forward. "We should move off the tarmac."

Rockley darted behind her legs and growled softly.

"Sorry," Caitlyn said at Glenn's sharp look, tugging the dog toward the plane. "He's still not comfortable around white men under forty." More specifically, a creepy frat boy who couldn't understand a woman not falling at his feet for a chance to sample his awesomeness.

"Is that your excuse too?" Glenn fell into step behind her as she trailed Lambert and his security detail. He'd asked her out repeatedly during the year since she'd started providing frequent hops between St. Isidore and the other Eastern Caribbean islands for his father.

Rather than take the hint each time she declined, he seemed only more intent on changing her mind.

"You know I don't date people I work with," she said. Even when they weren't self-important assholes.

He leaned close and whispered in her ear, his hand skimming down her back. "Make an exception. It'll be worth it."

Caitlyn's skin crawled and she jerked away as his hot breath touched her neck. "That's—"

"Come to the music festival in Sancoins with me this weekend," he cut in. "You'll have fun."

Sure, if one's idea of fun was getting date raped.

If Glenn had been her client, she would've turned down the steady work after the first flight, and damn the money. But he wasn't, and she didn't want to let him ruin what was otherwise a good thing, so she'd been reluctant to stir up trouble. But she should talk to Mr. Lambert, request that Glenn not accompany him on her plane anymore. "No, thank you," she said. "Nothing's changed."

His handsome face twisted into a scowl. "If you and this guy are so hot and heavy, how come he lives in DC and you're here?"

Kurt would probably laugh at the irony of her using his name to fend off unwanted advances, but she'd realized early on that it was better for business to pretend she was in a serious relationship. Fewer bruised egos and unwelcome propositions.

But her story had grown suspicious after so many years of "dating," so last month she'd faked an engagement. She now wore a modest CZ solitaire she'd ordered from the

Internet on her left ring finger.

"We're working on it," she said, skirting around Glenn. "He already popped the question, we just need to sort out the details."

"I'm starting to doubt this fiancé of yours is even real."

Her heart skipped. None of this was his business, and her story was supposed to convince him to back off.

Glenn followed on her heels. "I mean, if you were my girl, I'd make things happen a lot faster."

Never. She quit walking and faced him. "Please stop. I mean it."

A nasty expression crossed his face and she tensed.

"Glenn!" Lambert growled. "Leave her alone. She's working."

Color stained Glenn's cheeks and he flashed a scowl in his father's direction. Then, he spun on his heel and stalked toward the plane, passing his father without a word.

Caitlyn lightly touched the weapon holstered at her side and started breathing again. She wasn't helpless against assholes like him anymore. That didn't mean she welcomed the conflict. The less contact with Glenn, the better.

As she started walking again, a silver glint flashed at the edge of the jungle. Without thought, Caitlyn launched herself at Lambert. "Get down!"

She caught him around the middle and knocked him to the ground. The impact as she landed across his hips jarred her entire skeleton.

Crack. A rifle shot ruptured the air. Lambert's guards dropped to their knees. They formed a wall in front of him and Caitlyn and turned their firepower on the gunman's location.

Within seconds the barrage stopped, leaving behind a coppery, sulfur-scented haze and a ringing in her ears.

"We got him." Christophe turned to Lambert, his voice faint. "Sir, are you all right?"

Caitlyn scrambled off her client, her heart on double time. There was no blood on either of them, and Lambert's eyes were open, his gaze lucid as he pushed to sitting. *Thank God.*

The shock of adrenaline kept her on her knees. She couldn't trust her shaky limbs yet. Some people claimed that near-death experiences made them feel more alive. Her stomach violently rejected the notion.

She'd been shot at before. Hell, she'd lived in a hyper-vigilant state of awareness during—and for a while after—her deployment to Iraq, but *damn.* Despite—or maybe because of—Lambert's security measures, she'd never expected bullets to fly here. Somehow that made it worse.

Christophe moved in and waved her back so he could check his boss's condition while she scanned the airfield. Perimeter security goons rushed the downed shooter and scurried like ants to ensure the remaining area was safe.

Get up, Cait. With a deep breath, she stood and brushed dirt off her pants with trembling hands. Empty hands. She must have dropped Rockley's leash when she knocked down Lambert.

"Ro?" she called, turning in a circle, shading her eyes from fresh sunlight glimmering over the treetops. "Rockley!"

Her breath backed up in her chest. *Please.*

A yelp came from her right. The mutt cowered under the plane's fuselage, up against one of the wheel chocks.

"Oh, thank God." She nearly fell to her knees. Stumbling, she ran to the dog and dropped to the tarmac, hugging him with one arm and stroking his back. "What a good boy. I'm sorry," she murmured. "I love you, sweetie. I love you."

He whined and nuzzled her face.

Her heart finally found its rhythm and she took a deep breath, dropping her forehead to his. "*Jesus.*"

Behind her, someone cleared his throat. Rockley growled and ducked his head. So, Glenn then.

She stood and tried unsuccessfully to wipe Ro's black hairs off her white shirt and tan cargo pants before turning.

"You okay?" Glenn asked, his brows furrowed.

"Fine." She jerked her chin at Lambert, who stood in a huddle of his men. "Your dad?"

"A few bruises, but alive, thanks to you." His voice deepened with anger. Glenn might be an ass, but the attempt on his dad's life had pissed him off.

She shrugged off his words. "I could just as easily have been wrong."

"But you weren't. And everyone else missed it." He rubbed a shaky hand over his mouth and down his jaw. Maybe he was human after all. "What clued you in?"

"A reflection. A small spark of light. The guy clearly wasn't an expert."

"And that was enough?"

"It didn't belong, and I've seen it before." But she was not going to talk about Iraq. Certainly not with him. "Does your dad still want to go?" she asked.

Glenn sighed and gave her a visual inspection. "Of course."

"Don't we need to wait for the police?"

He gave her a "get real" look. "This is St. Isidore. He owns the police."

She managed not to frown. Lambert was a legitimate businessman. Sure, there'd been rumors, but she'd never seen anything to suggest that his dealings went beyond greasing the skids to get things done in some of the corrupt island-nations, something every businessman in the Caribbean undoubtedly did.

"The guards are handling things. If the cops need a statement," Glenn said, "they'll contact you later, but this was pretty straightforward. The other guy shot first."

"Any idea who it was?"

"Doesn't much matter now."

She shivered. It *did* matter. Someone wanted Treavor Lambert dead, and if the shooter had a boss, her client was still in danger. As was she by association.

"Woman of the year!" Lambert bellowed as he approached, wiping dust from the back of his suit jacket. "You saved me." He grabbed her free hand and pumped it between both of his.

"Just protecting my number one source of income." She gently slipped free of his grasp.

He laughed, deepening the creases etched into his deeply tanned face by the Caribbean sun. "I'll double it."

"Sir, that's not—"

"Nonsense." He didn't appear shaken, but then he was an expert at hiding behind bluster. "Don't argue with me. I'm the customer."

She wrangled a deferential smile. "Okay. Thank you."

Dropping his jubilant expression, he asked. "Are you okay? You good to fly?"

"One hundred percent," she said, grabbing for Rockley's leash. "Let's do it."

"Excellent. Come inside and get some coffee while I change into a clean suit." He pinched the shredded fabric of his pants between his fingertips. "This one is ruined."

Inside? She'd never been invited into his home before. "What about Rockley?"

"Bring him." Lambert waved her to follow him and then waited for her to catch up, leading her along a brick path toward the house.

She gave the leash a gentle tug and moved in alongside Lambert as they passed through a gate, and up to the wraparound porch held up by ornate columns.

After they entered through a set of French doors, he waved her toward a doorway. "Coffee's already made. Mugs, cream, and sugar are on the counter. One of the girls in there can help you. I'll be out in a few minutes."

"Thank you, sir."

Glenn had stayed outside talking to the guards, so she felt safe entering the kitchen alone. Whereas the living room had been appointed in ornate furnishings that looked too old and valuable to safely sit on, the kitchen was modern. As big as her small house, it was bright and airy with pale gray cabinets, stainless appliances, and white granite counter tops. A large window over the farmhouse sink and a skylight over the island let in the washed-out light of early morning.

To her left, a wide counter had been turned into a drink station with a coffee maker, cappuccino machine, and an electric tea kettle. "Something for everyone," she muttered. "Rockley, sit."

He followed her command and she pushed the looping handle of his leash down onto her forearm to free up her hands. Grabbing a yellow mug off a rack of hooks filled with a rainbow-colored set, she filled it about halfway and added a little cream and sugar.

Lambert would be out any minute. No need to take more than she could drink.

"Can I help you with anything, ma'am?" a familiar voice asked from behind her.

The mug slipped from Caitlyn's hands and shattered on the tile floor.

* * *

Rose looked as shocked as Caitlyn. "*Caity*?" she whispered, brown eyes wide. "How did you find me?"

"I didn't." All the searching she'd done since Rose had gone undercover nearly four months ago to help bring down a human trafficking ring, and her sister had been right here. Maybe the whole time. "I'm working. We came inside because —"

"Rose!" A gravelly female voice came from another room, sharp as broken glass. "What was that?"

Rose's eyes widened even more, eyebrows pinched in fear. All the color leached from beneath her warm, brown skin. "No," she mouthed to Caitlyn as she opened a pantry door. "A broken mug, ma'am. I'm cleaning it up now."

Dark bruises were visible on Rose's upper arms, and she'd corralled the tight curls of her rust-colored hair into a sleek bun at the back of her neck, revealing more bruising on her left jaw.

Oh, God. What had they done to her? Caitlyn glanced around, her stomach hollow. There had to be a way to get Rose out of here before she suffered another blow from whatever bastard had caused such pain.

"Mrs. Lambert is—" A wide-hipped black woman with short graying curls entered the kitchen and stopped at the sight of Caitlyn. "Oh. I didn't realize we had a visitor. I'm Reini, head housekeeper."

"Caitlyn Brevard," she managed without sounding too odd.

"Were you taking part in the target practice?"

Target practice? That would explain why neither of them was freaking out from the sounds of gunfire.

"Um, no. I'm Mr. Lambert's pilot. He needed a minute and offered me coffee." Caitlyn made a face somewhere between a smile and a grimace and tried to control her trembling limbs. Too much had happened in too little time for her to process. She pointed to the Pollock-like disaster of ceramic shards and coffee that Rose had already begun to sweep up. "I'm afraid I made a mess."

The older woman's gaze took in the scene, her nose twitching at the sight of Rockley, who was only refraining from licking the coffee because Caitlyn held his collar. If the woman had spared any thought to Caitlyn and Rose both having red hair and freckles, she didn't seem to understand the significance.

And why should Reini suspect anything? Beyond those typical redhead traits, the half-sisters looked nothing alike, their physical differences going far beyond skin tone. Rose's dad must have shared the recessive gene for red hair, but John Weekes was a short, wiry black man from Barbados, whereas Caitlyn's father was a tall, big-boned white guy from Chicago.

The only "type" their mother had, when it came to men, was the leaving kind.

Reini's pinched expression smoothed. "No problem, ma'am. We'll take care of it." She stepped around the spill to the far side of the island. "Would you like another cup of coffee?"

"No, thank you. I'm leaving in a minute."

"What's this?" Lambert's deep voice filled the room, shrinking the room to claustrophobic proportions.

"Just a mishap," Reini said. "We'll take care of it, sir."

Caitlyn's mind raced. She couldn't abandon Rose.

As if sensing her thoughts, her sister glanced up and gave a small shake of her head.

Fear etched Caitlyn's chest like acid, but she couldn't see a way to get Rose out of this place without them both getting shot. As much as it pained her, she had to retreat and return with a plan.

At least now she knew Rose was alive and where to find her. Not necessarily safe, but her situation could be much worse.

I'll come back for you.

Turning to face Lambert, she said, "Sorry. I dropped my mug."

"A few jitters are to be expected," he said, ever the gracious one. Except now she knew him for the heartless bastard he really was. "Are you sure you're good to fly?"

She gave a brisk nod and followed him out of the room, not allowing herself to look back. "Of course."

"Good." He smiled. "I'm running late for my meeting."

Her mind and body were numb with loss. Every leaden step took her further away from Rose. And her bruises. And whoever had delivered them. Caitlyn would like to return the favor.

God, *Rose*. Caitlyn forced herself to unclench her hands and breathe slowly.

Focus.

The excessive number of guards, the whispers surrounding Lambert's business dealings, his fast-growing fortune. It all made sense now.

And no wonder Rose hadn't escaped after a week or two undercover. She hadn't ended up in some random household from which she might sneak away, she'd landed in Lambert's secure compound surrounded by fences and men with rifles.

She hadn't stood a chance.

Caitlyn and Lambert were on the grass that edged the runway before he spoke again. "I discussed it with my wife, and we have a request. Our way of saying thanks for what you did today."

And she had to pretend her world hadn't been tossed. She cleared her throat and tried to pay attention. "What's that, sir?"

"You must come to Arielle's engagement party," he said. His youngest daughter was set to marry into one of the richest "high white" families on Barbados—descendants of the original plantation owners—in October. "And bring your fiancé. I want to meet the man who can handle such a firecracker." He winked.

Shit. Warning bells went off in her brain. "Oh, sir, I'm not sure—"

"No arguments." He stalked toward the plane, and the rest of his entourage followed. "If you've already booked clients for that evening I'll pay to have someone else take them. Tell your man to take a weekend off. Tell him it's *important*." She opened her mouth to protest and his expression turned hard as he looked over his shoulder. "No arguments. I'll see you both there."

Dammit. She had to get out of this. Maybe the police could help. Maybe none of this would matter after today.

He owns the police.

Glenn had straight up told her that.

To maintain her trusted position within his sphere—and find a way to help Rose and anyone else imprisoned behind his walls—she needed to pretend nothing was amiss.

And if the police failed her, she had to attend the party. With Kurt on her arm.

Trapped like a spider under a cat's paw, she swallowed hard. "Of course. We'd be honored."

CHAPTER TWO

KURT STEELE BREATHED OUT AND pressed the trigger, running through the steps of marksmanship on autopilot. Five shots, five holes in the paper target, center mass.

Six. *Dead on.* Seven.

Pain gripped his lower leg—well, where his lower leg used to be—and his shot went wild.

Next to him, Dan Molina lowered his weapon and gave Kurt a "what the hell was that?" smirk. Then his smile dropped and he tapped his earmuffs before removing them.

Kurt lifted the protection from one ear, forcing himself to stand tall as he took deep breaths through his nose.

"You okay, man?"

"Fine." Sometimes his friends read him too well. "Just lost focus."

"Bullshit. You could take that shot in your sleep."

"It's nothing. Sometimes I still get...twinges." Phantom pain, twinges, whatever.

"*Twinges.*" Dan's voice was laced with skepticism, maybe concern.

Kurt let the earmuff drop, dismissing his friend, who also worked for him at Steele Security. There were advantages to being the boss.

Talking wasn't going to help anything, and the pain was already diminishing. After six years, he knew how to work through it, and the inexplicable sensations didn't last as long or come as frequently as they had early on.

He raised his weapon and fired. Eight. Center mass. *That's more like it.*

The range was quiet midmorning on a Tuesday. He and Dan and the owner were the only people around.

They ran through their ammo and pulled in their final targets. Kurt had to get back to the office for an eleven o'clock meeting, and it would be at least a twenty-minute drive to Arlington.

"Nice grouping," a woman said from behind him.

He holstered his Beretta and faced her. "Detective Breschi. I'm sure yours would look similar."

"Thanks, but I wish you'd call me Eva." He might be out of practice when it came to dating, but even he couldn't miss the way she leaned in and maintained eye contact, or the hint of a suggestive smile on her wide lips.

"I know." But he wouldn't.

Her smile slipped and she turned away, showing off her tight ass in form-fitting black slacks. "Dan, good to see you." She chose a spot further down the range, leaving behind a faint cloud of perfume.

As soon as they were paid up and outside in the cool October air, Dan attacked. "Dude, the pretty detective *so* wants you. Why don't you at least take her out for dinner? See how it goes."

Kurt shook his head and put on his sunglasses. "She doesn't want me. She wants to prove to herself she's a patriot by fucking a wounded warrior."

Dan glanced back at the building, his expression skeptical. "What makes you say that?"

"Experience."

"Shit. Sorry." Dan took a few steps in silence. "But still. Is that necessarily a bad thing?"

"I have no desire to be her charity case." God save him from well-meaning friends who were happily married now.

"But if it gets you laid…" Dan leaned against the minivan he and Alyssa had bought after Sophie was born last July. "Let's say patriotism or some sense of, I don't know, *altruism* is her motivation. How is it any different from hooking up with a spec ops groupie?"

Sometimes friends and their long memories were a pain in the ass. "Because I'm not twenty-four anymore. And I had legs back then. Those women worshiped our strength. They thought of us as heroes, and they wanted some of that to rub off on them." Or against them, anyway.

Dan rubbed his dark stubble. "I'm pretty sure Eva thinks you're a hero."

Kurt scoffed. "Losing your legs isn't heroic. It's just plain-ass bad luck."

"Whatever." Dan opened his car door. "If you're not into her, I get it. But it wouldn't kill you to have a little fun."

"I'm a ball of fun."

Dan grinned and shook his head. "I'll see you tomorrow, *boss*." He, Todd, and Jason were working security at the Ritz in Tysons Corner this evening for the wedding of a congresswoman's daughter.

Kurt watched his friend drive off before getting into his truck. Maybe Dan was right, but he couldn't muster any enthusiasm for the idea.

Half an hour later, he entered Steele Security's office on

the fifth floor of a high-rise building in Arlington. The main lobby of the suite had a floor-to-ceiling window with a view of the Potomac, the Lincoln Memorial, and the Washington Monument that never grew old.

From behind a counter-height mahogany desk, Tara Fujimoto—aka the world's best business manager—looked up and greeted him with a smile. "Hey. How was the range?"

"I killed the target."

She flipped her long black hair off her shoulder. "Oh, good. We're safe for another day." Reaching for a small stack of paper, she said, "Scott called. Everything went well at Valerie's ultrasound appointment."

"Boy or girl?"

"No idea. They want it to be a surprise."

Between his sister and half of his team over the last few years, it seemed as if everyone was having babies. Would he ever get to be a dad? Thirty-four wasn't exactly ancient, but he hadn't been on a date in years. Kind of hard to become a father when you're celibate.

"Also, Caitlyn Brevard is in the break room with Todd," Tara said, with no knowledge that she'd just dropped a bomb. "She wanted to know if you could fit her in today."

"She's *here*?" Kurt pointed at the floor, feeling thick in the head, even as his heart galloped.

"Yeah. She's been waiting about ten minutes. Todd arrived early for your meeting and offered to get her a cup of coffee."

I'll bet he did. According to Jason, when Caitlyn had helped out on a mission for Steele a few years back, Todd had followed her around as if attached by a leash. Jason had ribbed Todd about it for months afterward. Kurt had worn the enamel from his back teeth trying to pretend he didn't give a shit.

"Thanks." Steeling himself to face her in person for the first time in twelve years, he squared his shoulders and turned toward the break room.

At the same moment, Caitlyn emerged with a ceramic mug in her left hand, and stopped several feet away. His heart skittered to a halt at the sight of her.

It shriveled and died when the large diamond ring on her left finger caught the overhead lights.

Caitlyn's stomach cartwheeled at her first sight of Kurt.

He was more intimidating than she remembered, his expression darker, his muscles more defined—if that were even possible. The contours of his familiar, handsome face had become more rugged, more sharply honed, more deeply carved. More beautiful.

She hadn't expected seeing him again to make her…*want*. He shouldn't have this effect on her, especially after so many years. There was no place for it in her life.

Ruthlessly shoving aside the messy feelings wreaking havoc on her system, she said goodbye to Todd and followed Kurt down the hall to his office, her feet sinking into the plush, brown carpet.

Kurt's appearance wasn't the only change. His gait was different too. Tighter, more constrained, less fluid and graceful. According to his company website, he was a disabled veteran. Whatever had happened to him, it had to be bad. She couldn't imagine him leaving the PJs—Air Force pararescuemen—willingly.

Business must be good, though. The rent on this place had to cost a fortune. His office had the same incredible view of the National Mall and the monuments as the lobby and was probably intended to impress the type of clients who were willing to drop wads of money on security.

He closed the door behind him and gestured her to a metal-framed chair. He rounded his desk and sat, his own chair squeaking in protest. Apparently not everything at Steele was top notch.

His wary brown eyes—so dark they almost appeared black—met hers across the desk. "It's good to see you, Caitlyn, but why are you here?"

So, no small talk then. She pried her hands apart and laid them on her thighs. "I have kind of an odd favor to ask."

"O-kay," he said, drawing out the word. "You know I'll help if I can."

She *had* known. That was the thing about Kurt. He didn't know how to refuse someone in need. It was both his greatest strength and the thing that drove her nuts about him, because he couldn't walk away even when the person didn't want his assistance.

She tilted her head and adopted a neutral expression, trying to recall the words she'd rehearsed in her head for days. "I have a regular client, Treavor Lambert. He's a big deal in the islands, with his hands in several businesses. When he needs to fly within the EC—the Eastern Caribbean—he calls me. For several reasons, I can't afford to lose him as a customer."

Kurt had leaned forward and now studied her intently. His thick eyebrows came together, but he said nothing.

She raised her chin. Not that he had any right, but if Kurt was anything like he used to be—Mr. Overprotective—he was going to flip his lid. Which was exactly why she hadn't led with her work for The Underground.

Though, to be fair, Kurt had brought her in for several missions that put her under fire in the last few years, so maybe he'd changed.

"For the last six months," she said, "I've been running

rescue flights for victims of human trafficking, mostly on St. Isidore." The island country's recovering economy had created demand for cheap labor and sex workers, and traffickers had stepped in to fill both needs. "There are people on the ground who go into brothels and warehouses and other businesses to help victims escape to a designated pickup point, and I fly in to get them."

"Sounds dangerous." Instead of judgment or misplaced protectiveness, his rich voice held only friendly concern laced with approval. "But I'm sure the people you help are grateful."

She stared at him for a beat. She'd been poised to defend her choices, to point out the hypocrisy of a guy who used to drop into hot zones to save wounded soldiers calling what she did dangerous. His response threw her off balance, as if she'd been pushing against a door that had suddenly opened without warning. "So far, I haven't had any trouble."

"How'd you get involved?"

"Last year, the graphic design company my sister Rose— technically my half-sister—worked for went out of business, and she decided to visit me in Barbados to see her dad's homeland. He's the one who got me interested in living there in the first place," she added as an aside. "Anyway, while there, she fell in love with a woman who runs STOP, an organization that raises awareness for, and helps the victims of, human trafficking and indentured servitude in the Caribbean."

"And sponsors these rescue flights?"

"Right. STOP needed a pilot who was up for a little risk. I was available and willing."

The muscle in his jaw gave a tic. "What does that have to do with your client? And me?"

Her stomach knotted. "Four months ago, Rose decided to

go undercover. Most of the trafficking victims are terrified of testifying against their abusers, and she thought she could go in, see how the system works, gather evidence and punch out in a week, maybe two. She answered several ads for housekeepers on St. Isidore, and finally got a response that seemed likely to be a scam, so she flew to St. Isidore for the job. She hasn't communicated with anyone since."

"Jesus. Four months?" Kurt rubbed his chin and stared out the window for a minute. "What about the cops?"

"I reported her missing, but corruption in St. Isidore's police force is still common. They could be getting paid to turn a blind eye. The government might even consider indentured servants a necessary measure to get the country back on its feet. People are trafficked for everything from sex work to manual labor and construction. I wouldn't be surprised if some of the politicians are involved or getting kickbacks to stay quiet."

"So you need someone to find her. My guys are good at that, and you know several of them have experience on St. Iz."

Caitlyn couldn't hold back an impatient head shake, but it wasn't his fault he didn't understand. "No. I know where she is. Three days ago, I found her—completely by accident—at Lambert's house, but security was too tight for me to get her out safely."

"Lambert, your client?"

She scowled. "Yeah." Finding out Treavor Lambert was a snake had cut deep. She'd liked the guy, in spite of the son he'd raised.

"Did you have any idea he was involved in this stuff?"

"None." And how had she missed it? Then again, it wasn't like Lambert had asked her to transport his victims. How would she have known?

"Well, since you know where Rose is, that makes our job easier. It's just a rescue operation."

"I'm not asking you to send any of your guys." She forced her hands onto her lap and rushed her explanation. "Lambert's plantation is heavily guarded. If you storm the place, too many people could get hurt. Not to mention it could cause an international incident. But now I literally have an engraved invitation into Lambert's house. Which is where you come in," she said. "I've been invited to an engagement party for his daughter." Caitlyn took a deep breath. *Just spit it out.* "It would be incredibly helpful if you could come to the party as my fiancé." She clamped her lips shut and waited.

"Your fiancé?" He gave her a what-the-hell look, and spots of color appeared on his cheeks. "Don't you have one of those already?"

Oh, no. He thought— God, could this be any more awkward? Why on earth hadn't she made up a name instead of using his?

Because Glenn would check.

"The ring is fake. To keep guys away."

Kurt's expression shuttered and he gave a slight shake of his head. "So why can't you just tell the police you found Rose and have them get a warrant?"

"Shaylee—Rose's girlfriend—tried. She contacted a cop in St. Isidore who she thinks is clean, but the woman said the people who could approve such an action are likely on Lambert's payroll. All we'd be doing is alerting him that I know Rose and want to rescue her. I need his trust."

With a sigh, Kurt wiggled the mouse on his desktop and then typed on his keyboard. "What are the dates? I'll check the calendar and see who's available to go with you."

Damn, damn, damn. She'd known this wouldn't be easy. She sat taller and cleared her throat. "Um, actually, I already gave Mr. Lambert your name."

Kurt froze, and then he leveled a dark look at her, his inky eyes unforgiving. "Why the hell would you do that?"

It was a fair question. She took another fortifying breath. "For years I've been telling people I'm in a long-distance relationship. I started because it helps me fend off advances from clients, but Lambert's son Glenn is a little…let's call him persistent. At some point he got suspicious and started pressing for details. I think he honestly can't understand a woman rejecting him." She grimaced involuntarily.

Kurt's lips thinned and he stared at her, waiting for her to continue.

"I wouldn't have bothered to provide specifics except that I see him frequently," she said. "I hoped if he thought my boyfriend was real, he'd back off. But he's the kind of guy who would verify my story, so I gave him your name and told him we had been dating a few years. Recently, I elevated your status to fiancé—" she wiggled her left ring finger, showing off the faux diamond ring "—hoping that if he thought we were more serious he'd finally get the hint and back off."

"Did he?"

She sighed. "Not really."

"Why me? Why not Terrell?" Kurt asked, his voice sharp as a talon.

As her closest friend, Terrell Washington would have been the obvious choice. The three of them had once been inseparable. "Because he was in a serious relationship with Selena already. If Glenn or his dad checked my story, I didn't want it to fall apart that easily."

"And what if I had started dating someone?"

"It was a risk, but last time I flew Dan and Alyssa to St. Isidore, Dan said you weren't seeing anyone and hadn't dated for a while." She cringed internally.

"You've been keeping track of my *love life*? Or the lack thereof." He flipped a pencil across the desk, his voice laced with bitterness.

"I'm sorry," she said, softly. "I never thought it would go this far. But now I've been invited, practically ordered, to attend this party and to bring you. I think both Glenn and his dad want proof that I'm not lying to them. Glenn because he's obsessive and cocky, and his dad because he wants to know he can trust me. If I show up alone, it throws my integrity into question."

Kurt stared at his fingers, his face impassive. After several seconds, he asked, "Why would a client invite you to this kind of family event?"

Not the question she'd expected. "Because I saved his life."

His thick eyebrows rose. "How?"

"I knocked him out of the way of sniper fire."

"Christ."

Caitlyn shrugged. "It was instinct. I'm not even sure the guy's life was worth saving." She'd had a lot of time to think about it after the initial rush of success. Had she been able to ignore her gut, or just drop to the ground to save her own hide, it might've solved everything. "Then again, that's when I was invited inside and found Rose."

If Lambert had died, would Rose have been set free? Probably not. After all, Glenn would take over, and he was as bad as his father, if not worse.

"You couldn't let him die any more than you could stop yourself from breathing," Kurt said with a hint of a smile. "There's a reason we called you Braveheart."

Caitlyn looked away from his intense gaze. The sun shone on DC, making the monuments glow against the backdrop of red and yellow trees, but even in October it was already far too cold for her taste. The sooner she got back to Barbados the better.

The squeak of Kurt's chair drew her attention. He leaned back to look at the ceiling, hands clasped behind his head in a way that showcased his impressive biceps. An unwelcome shock of desire bolted down her spine.

"I know I'm asking a lot," she said. "And I know that it's even more awkward given our history. But I wouldn't expect you to do this for free. I can hire you."

"No you can't." He dropped his hands and sat forward, propping his forearms against the desk. "This isn't about money. Never mind that I have a business to run, there's a reason I don't work in the field. There are things you don't know about me that could change your mind." He sighed. "And if I did say yes, there are things we need to hash out, because there's no way I can act like a loving fiancé to you right now."

All she could do was nod. She was the one who needed his help, so she would do whatever he wanted, no matter how painful. "I know you were injured. I know it had to be serious for the Air Force to medically retire you." She almost dreaded knowing. Dreaded the thought of him being hurt... "Will you tell me what happened?"

Kurt pushed his chair away from the desk and stood, pausing for a second before he walked around. He stared at her for several heartbeats, the muscle in his jaw jumping. "I was on a call in Helmand Province when our bird took a hit." He lifted the hems of his pants to reveal black plastic and shiny metal where his legs should have been. "This happened."

CHAPTER THREE

EVERY MUSCLE IN KURT'S BODY tensed as he prepared for Caitlyn's reaction.

"Oh, shit," she blurted at the sight of his prosthetics.

He dropped his pant legs. "I was one of the lucky ones." The shock and pity and sorrow in her eyes wouldn't gut him if she were anyone else.

Her lips pursed. She took a deep, shaky breath, squared her shoulders, and gave him a slow once-over that might have heated his blood under other circumstances. Setting her hands on her hips, she said, "Seems like you're taking this whole *Man of Steele* thing a bit far."

He blinked.

Then he laughed as a relieved breath tumbled out of him at her use of the nickname that wouldn't die. "Yeah, I guess so. Though technically, it's titanium and aluminum…"

Holy hell, she was perfect. No tears, no apologies, no angry tirades about the unfairness of the world, no questions about why he bothered to get out of bed in the morning. Just humor. Just his old friend who still understood exactly what he needed.

Except he had to check the impulse to kiss her right now. Though, really, that wasn't a *new* problem.

Her emerald eyes—yes, emerald, goddammit, green as the pendant his mother had worn every day—met his, and his stomach bottomed out. Twelve years since he'd last seen her, and she was even more beautiful than he remembered. Freckles still spattered every inch of skin bared by her V-neck T-shirt, and her auburn hair was pulled into a twist, the way she'd worn it in the Air Force. She still wore confidence as a second skin too.

She bit her lower lip and his mind took off into dangerous territory. "So you think you can't do the job because of this," she said, her voice flat as she gestured to his legs.

Her words slammed him back to reality with a sickening thud. "Yes." Jesus, no need to belabor the point.

"But you're running a business, so your brain's okay, right?" she asked. "No TBI?" Traumatic brain injury was common among vets, especially those who'd suffered catastrophic injuries. Her concern had merit.

"No. I got lucky there. There was no explosion, and my helmet did its job."

She grimaced and gave a sharp nod. "How's your aim?"

"Probably still not as good as yours, but I do all right." In their Air Force days, she'd been the best shot in the maintenance squadron, and probably the best on base. More than a few of her ex-boyfriend Aaron's Security Forces buddies had lost their dignity by betting against her at the range.

"Great. I don't expect any trouble, but just in case…"

An exasperated grunt escaped him. "You don't get it. Unlike many amputees—even some of the older veterans—

I'm lucky enough that Uncle Sam gives me the most advanced prosthetics money can buy. I'm highly functional. But I don't have the tactical mobility to be effective in the face of a threat."

"I'm not hiring you for security. But if I were, it would be for your strategic mind. Your ability to create a plan and anticipate problems. That's your real strength." She waved her hand down his body like one of those game show models on *The Price is Right*, an appreciative expression on her face that made his skin tingle. "I mean, you're obviously strong…"

Her green eyes met his and he could almost imagine he saw desire there. Could almost imagine leaning in, pressing her to the wall, and— He gave himself a mental head shake. She'd made his "friend status" clear a long time ago in the worst possible way.

But he couldn't pull his gaze away from her mouth, from the little freckle that perched on the line at the edge of her upper lip.

Jesus. This was such a bad idea. He'd totally lied. He'd have zero trouble pretending to be the besotted fiancé. But playing the role, knowing she didn't reciprocate, would be pure hell.

And yet, how could he say no? He'd never been able to walk away from a friend in need. If she was just doing this to fend off an overzealous admirer, he'd tell her to shove it. But, one, this guy Glenn sounded more like potential stalker material, and two, her cause was just. If helping her meant saving innocent lives, not to mention her sister… What choice did he have?

Fuuuck. "If I'm going to agree to this, we need to set some ground rules. The first being that you find yourself a new fake boyfriend once the party is over."

Caitlyn looked as if she'd eaten something bitter. "Fair

enough."

"But before that, I think we need to clear the air."

"Unfortunately, I'm tied up all afternoon. Can you be back here at five?" Kurt asked, his expression making it clear that *never* would be preferable.

"Of course. I know I sprang this on you, but I'm flying home in the morning, so I'll be as flexible as you need."

Caitlyn killed the time with a six-mile run around the Mall and monuments that did nothing to calm her nerves, a late lunch at a deli in Arlington, and a short, fitful nap in her hotel room before returning to Steele's offices.

"Hi," Tara Fujimoto said with a smile from behind the massive reception desk when Caitlyn entered. "I'll let Kurt know you're here."

"Thanks."

Caitlyn had met Tara briefly a few years ago. According to Todd Brennan—one of Kurt's guys—she was Steele's receptionist, business manager, supply ninja, and team mom, rolled into one. And she somehow did it all while looking as if she'd just stepped out of the pages of one of the fashion magazines Caitlyn's mom still read from cover to cover.

Tara was too short to be a model—maybe five feet out of those towering heels she wore—but she was petite, polished, and beautiful, with long, glossy black hair, wearing a tailored blue dress that was both professional and sexy.

Next to her, Caitlyn probably looked freakishly tall and drab in her V-neck and jeans with running shoes, hair pulled off her face. But, as a pilot, comfort—especially given the Caribbean's humidity—and deflecting unwanted interest were her top fashion priorities. Besides, even if she made an effort, she couldn't compete with a woman like Tara. Caitlyn had inherited none of her mom's sense of style.

Which was fine. She'd rather not waste the energy.

"Can I get you anything to drink?" Tara asked, after she'd spoken to Kurt over the intercom.

Caitlyn declined and sat on the long, brown sofa, laying her parka over the armrest. Magazines were artfully scattered across a low, glass coffee table: *Foreign Affairs*, *Guns & Ammo*, *Men's Health*. Tara returned to her work and the office was silent, save for the heat blowing through the overhead vent and the tapping of a keyboard.

Five minutes later, as Caitlyn thumbed through an old issue of *The Economist*, Kurt emerged from the hallway behind a tall, thin black man who towered over Kurt's six feet. The man buttoned his suit coat and slung a leather messenger bag across his chest.

"Thanks for walking me through everything, Gordon," Kurt said.

"No problem. I should have the paperwork ready for your signature early next week."

"Perfect. Enjoy your weekend."

"You too." The man waved to Tara and left the office.

Kurt stopped at Tara's desk. "You don't have to stay. I can close up."

"I know," she said, with a quick smile. "But I want to finish double-checking the numbers before I release everyone's payments on Monday morning." She glanced at Caitlyn and pitched her voice too low to hear from across the room.

He shook his head. "No. Nothing like that. I just thought you might want an early start on the weekend."

"I don't think Netflix will mind if I'm running a little late. Might as well get this done so I'm not stressing over it."

Netflix? In her interactions with the people at Steele, Tara had struck Caitlyn as a social creature. One who would always have a date or a night out with friends on her calendar. But what did she know? Maybe Tara was one of those super-friendly introverts who retreated to her home at the end of the day to recharge in solitude.

Now *that* Caitlyn could understand.

"I appreciate it," Kurt said. "But remember, there are no bonus points for being a workaholic around here."

"Thanks, Pot."

He chuckled. "Sure thing, Kettle."

Aww, weren't they flippin' adorable? Caitlyn feigned interest in the magazine on her lap. Could she be disrupting a fledgling relationship with her request? Kurt and Tara would be beautiful together, but the thought left a sour taste in her mouth. Which was stupid. She had no right to be jealous, especially since she had no desire to get romantically entangled with a man she couldn't walk away from, no matter how sexy.

A long-term man was not part of her long-term plan.

Kurt turned to her, his smile fading. "Ready?"

Never. "Sure." She grabbed her coat and followed him to his office. Through the east-facing window, the low sun washed the Capitol in gold, setting the colorful trees aflame. "Your view is incredible."

He gazed out over the Potomac. "I like it, though I'm sure it's nothing compared to the view from your office."

The view from her cockpit *was* tough to beat. "A little variety is good." She hung her jacket on a rack near the door and slid into the same seat she'd taken earlier.

Kurt settled across the desk from her and rearranged a stack of papers. "So…"

Might as well get to it. She let out a deep breath. "I'm sorry I didn't ask permission, or at least warn you that I'd used your name. I honestly never expected it to matter, but I figured if Lambert did follow up, you'd be both legit and intimidating." She caught herself wringing her hands and clasped them together in her lap. *Be strong.* "As much as I love Terrell, even if he was single, Glenn would never believe I was dating a guy who owns a comic book store in Maine."

Kurt studied her, his expression unreadable, not leaving even the tiniest crack in his mask from which to gauge his thoughts.

She swallowed hard. "Besides, there are very few people I trust in this world, and you're still one of them."

"Unfortunately, I can't say the same about you."

The air rushed from her lungs. Wow, direct hit. But then, she deserved it, didn't she? "I'm sorry for how I treated you."

He twiddled a pencil between two fingers, but his eyes never left her face. "I get deciding you're not ready for a serious relationship, especially with a guy who's staring down nearly two years of training. And I know all we did was kiss before I left, but after two years of being friends, it felt significant. Like the start of something. I spun foolish, elaborate fantasies around you while I was gone, and you were back at Tinker fucking other men."

Her cheeks flamed. The urge to defend herself rose hot and eager as lava in a volcano, but she tamped it down. No matter how much it hurt him, she'd rather he believed the lie.

"At *any* point during the ten weeks I was at Indoc," he said, his voice unexpectedly soft, "you could have told me you didn't plan to wait around."

That hadn't been her plan at all, but telling him so would only confuse things. "I didn't want to distract you, but I know I could have handled it better. I'm sorry."

His mouth twisted.

Did he want her to be more contrite? More apologetic? There was no point. She couldn't change what she'd done.

He'd either get past it or not.

"Why did you even kiss me then?"

Her stomach dipped. Kissing him had been like sipping champagne. Delicious and sparkling and fun, and so, so hard to stop. She looked down at her hands intertwined in her lap.

Something had changed in her that night. They'd been waiting outside after dinner at a popular Mexican restaurant in Oklahoma City while Terrell used the restroom. Kurt had leaned against his battered Explorer, hands in his shorts pockets, looking hotter than ever after all the workouts he'd done to prep for PJ training. And it hit her.

He was leaving.

She'd kept him at arm's length for the two years since he'd joined their maintenance crew, initially because she was dating Aaron, a cop on base, and later because they were coworkers. And, ultimately, because he was the kind of man she could fall for too easily. Smart, fun, handsome, honorable to a fault, and sexy as hell. But Caitlyn hadn't wanted to fall. Not ever again.

She would not be her mother, who repeatedly gave away her heart, gave away her power to men, and received nothing but misery in return. Caitlyn would no longer allow herself to be that emotionally vulnerable.

But that night, she'd wanted a taste of Kurt, of what she was missing out on. A little piece of him to carry with her when he was gone.

"I don't know," she finally said, because how did you ever explain the magnetic draw of another person? And why you would run from it. "You were leaving and I wanted to know what it would be like." Could she come up with a more pathetic answer? When it came down to it, she'd been selfish.

His lips curled. "Not good enough, apparently."

God, that he could doubt his appeal. "You're a great

kisser." In fact, part of her wouldn't mind a repeat right now. "I just can't do long term, and I sensed that you wanted more." That wasn't entirely untrue. "I wasn't ready for that. I'll probably never be ready. I'm sorry I didn't handle it better."

"Me too." Kurt sighed and gave a slight head shake. "This is ridiculous. It's been twelve years. I should be able to move past something that happened when I was twenty-fucking-two years old."

She scoffed. "If you learn how, let me know."

His eyes narrowed at her slip.

Rushing in before he could question her, she said, "I'm not asking you to forgive me, just to give me a chance now." She stared at her hands. The cold weather and artificial heat had already dried her cuticles and caused a hangnail.

"Because you need a fake fiancé."

"Yes." She took a deep breath and bit her lip. "But also because I've missed you."

He scoffed. "You don't have to lay it on so thick."

Of course he thought she was trying to manipulate him. In all fairness, she was. But not just to save Rose. Time had given her perspective. She could see now how much she'd hurt them both. To protect herself, she'd hurt him instead.

Deep down, maybe that was why she hadn't considered any alternatives to this plan. Because she finally had an excuse to meet with him face to face and work things out.

Bracing her hands on her knees, she leaned forward. "If you really can't do this for me, I'll suck it up and say we broke things off. It was selfish to think I could waltz in here and ask this of you." She sat back. "But either way, I'd like to try to be friends again."

"Why?" he asked, the bafflement in his voice tugging at her heart.

Why indeed? This wasn't her plan at all. "Because I like you?"

He gave an exasperated laugh and shook his head. "You're not selling this very well, Brevard."

She shrugged. "Hey, I'm a bit rusty. Normally, I just hang out with my dog. He doesn't care what I say as long as I feed him."

"You have a dog?" A full-on smile lit Kurt's handsome face, and something in her chest fluttered.

She ruthlessly crushed it. *We're friends.* Or they might be again, eventually. Anything more was out of the question. He could so easily hold all the power in the relationship if she gave in to her inconveniently alert libido. Her aversion to that wouldn't change, and she didn't want to hurt him again. "Yep."

"Me too. A German Shepherd. In fact, I need to get home to feed Max and let him out." Kurt laid his big, strong hands on the desk, his smile slipping away. "So tell me this. If we 'break up,' what happens with Glenn and his father? And Rose."

She sighed. "I don't know. I'll think of something. It's not so far-fetched that we might end things. If you and I were actually engaged, I can't imagine trying to decide who'd give up their business to live with the other. After three years, it's the perfect excuse to call it quits."

"As long as you don't say I cheated."

Her heart sank. He was going to beg off. "I would never impugn your character that way," she said. That was one thing his future wife wouldn't have to worry about. Kurt was a man of honor to his core.

He rubbed his forehead. "You figured I wouldn't be able to turn you down, didn't you?"

Damn. She'd totally miscalculated. "I'll admit, I hoped

your savior complex might work in my favor." She sent him an apologetic smile. Suddenly it was vital that he not feel coerced into helping her. "But you owe me nothing. We were friends once, I was stupid, maybe we can be friends again. If you agree to do this and resent me later, it's not worth it."

The sentiment surprised her as much as it seemed to shock him. She'd flown to DC determined to convince Kurt any way she could, but with him sitting right in front of her, she couldn't bring herself to guilt him into helping her with a problem she alone had created.

"Just how far would we have to take this ruse?" he asked, his dark eyes probing.

Heat rose up her neck and warmed her face, even as her heart kicked with hope. "Some light PDA for authenticity, like holding hands, maybe a quick kiss here and there." Her stomach flipped at the last thought. Jesus. Would she be able to keep the public displays of affection under control? She unconsciously licked her lips and his eyes followed the motion. Her body tingled in anticipation. Maybe this was a horrible idea. "You okay with that?"

One side of his mouth kicked up. "I think I can handle it."

But could she? "Does that mean you're on board?"

He sighed. "I'll have to check my calendar, but yeah. When do you need me?"

Right now. Given her way, she'd straddle him on the chair and kiss him blind. Or at least pump her fist in triumph. She refrained from both. "In two weeks. The party's on Saturday, the twenty-first."

The wait to get to Rose was going to be excruciating, but she didn't see another way to save her without causing a political shit storm and getting a lot of people hurt or killed, possibly innocents.

He donned a pair of reading glasses that somehow made him even sexier, and clicked his computer mouse several times, his expression inscrutable. "Fine. I'll do it."

CHAPTER FOUR

TALKING TO CAITLYN NEARLY EVERY day was going to kill him. Kurt didn't want to like her, laugh with her, remember she was human. Or worse, fall under her spell again.

He had nixed video calls, claiming that he wanted to talk while walking Max or cooking dinner, but he was more worried about her reading every lustful expression as it crossed his face.

And if she smiled, he might just short circuit.

So now, he walked his neighborhood in the chilly dark on the first night after she'd returned home, phone in his front pocket. His headphones had a built-in microphone, and he had one earbud in place, the other tucked under his shirt collar so he could maintain situational awareness.

"How's Sara?" Caitlyn asked about his sister.

"Great. She became a nurse like my parents, and she married my physical therapist about four years ago," Kurt said as he tugged Max's leash to get him moving again. Lampposts were the dog's favorite target.

"Wow. Was that awkward?"

More than it should have been. "It was a little weird for me when they started dating, but I wasn't Soham's patient by that point, and he's a great guy. A good dad. They have a three-year-old named Luke."

"I'll bet you're a good uncle."

"The best."

She chuckled and his chest tightened.

"That kid pretty much hangs the moon as far as I'm concerned. I spoil him mercilessly." After all, Luke was the closest thing to having a son of his own he might ever get.

"Evil man."

"It's a brother's duty to torment his sister."

Caitlyn was silent for a few seconds. Had they been disconnected? "Mine never really got the chance."

"You have a brother?" Jesus. Had he ever really known her?

"Mike was ten when I left home. He and Rose have the same dad. John Weekes. He reminisced about Barbados incessantly, and painted such an enticing picture that it became my dream to move here."

"And you did."

"Yeah."

"Are he and your mom still married?"

"No. She has a boyfriend now. Paul," she said as if her mom had shacked up with a cockroach.

"That bad, huh?"

She sighed. "Probably not. I just think she gives herself away too easily. She's beautiful and smart, but she never finished high school. So, these guys offer her a bit of financial security and she thinks she loves them. Unfortunately, they only love the idea of her, not the messy reality. Beauty only gets you so far."

"That sucks."

"Yeah, well. Could be worse. They never hit her or mistreated us kids. And we always had a roof over our heads and food on the table. I just thought…"

Kurt waited her out.

"When I joined the Air Force, I thought if I left home, lightened her burden, she might not need to rely on someone else anymore. Especially if I sent home most of my paycheck."

"What happened?"

"She refused the money. But at least she stopped marrying the men after John. I felt bad for Rose and Mike getting shuffled from house to house, one guy to another, and maybe guilty for getting out."

"None of that's your fault." But he'd probably feel the same. Hell, he felt guilty now for having a better childhood. His parents had been strict but fair, madly in love, and stable. His only worry growing up had been disappointing them.

"Sure." Pots clanged in the background and she swore under her breath. "Are your parents still traveling the world saving people?"

"No." The claws of grief were no longer so sharp, but they still clung. "They were killed in a bus crash in Honduras eight years ago."

"Oh, no. I'm sorry."

"Yeah."

"Were they on vacation?"

"Working," he said, trying to push away the selfish anger that rose up whenever he thought about it. When he'd finally needed them, his parents were gone. Childish, but there it was. "They were there with an NGO to provide medical aid, but they never made it to the camp."

"Damn."

That about summed it up.

Kurt extended his walk to the next neighborhood, reluctant to take her voice into his home where he might never get it out.

"We should probably come up with a story about how we started dating," she said after a long moment of silence. "And make up a few visits over the last few years."

He'd rather eat cat food. "That's easy enough. We stick to the truth. I called you three years ago to help out my team on St. Isidore and we started talking again. We'll have to whitewash it a bit because I don't want anybody to connect my team to the dead rebels."

"I think hiring me to fly them off the island is enough. And then we decided to meet up in DC to reminisce about our glory days as AWACS maintainers?"

"Sure." Kurt had loved being a mechanic for the E-3 AWACS—basically, a Boeing 707 topped with a rotating radar dome, that provided air traffic control from the sky—but he'd loved being a PJ more. "We met up and things developed from there." Things like kissing and touching and loving. *Fuck.*

Yeah, that too, if he had his way.

"That's a little vague," she said.

Exactly. Kurt stopped walking and took several deep breaths. *Get it together.* "You plan to share details with Glenn?"

"Uh, no. But people at parties, especially engagement parties, love to share how-they-met stories. I just thought we should have a few more details figured out in case anyone asks."

"Go for it." Why had he agreed to this torture again?

"Okay. We spent the day at the Air & Space museum, because we're total stereotypes."

"The main one, or Udvar-Hazy?" he asked, just to be contrary.

"I've only been to the one on the Mall."

"Okay. We met at the museum in DC," he said, fully able to imagine spending a day surrounded by flying machines, chatting with her as if they hadn't set fire to their friendship. "Then what?"

"Neither of us wanted the day to end, so we took the Metro to Georgetown for dinner at a little Italian restaurant near the Potomac."

"And then?" he asked, feeling a little breathless.

"Since we're sticking close to the truth, I kissed you outside the restaurant after dinner."

Unh. Direct hit. As if it had happened yesterday, he could feel her lips on his when she'd completely blindsided him outside a restaurant in Oklahoma City. After two years of pretending he was fine just being friends, that soft, warm, *deep* kiss had hit him like an IED. Total annihilation.

"And then we got a hotel room because getting to my house in Fairfax would take too long," he said, giving them the ending to the evening he'd always wanted.

"Wow. Straight from idle to full afterburners. You move fast."

He hadn't moved fast enough. He forced a smile, hoping it would make his words come out more playful. "Didn't you know Easy is my middle name?"

She laughed then, a bright, unexpected sound that scorched his soul. "Your parents could have been much cleverer. Stainless. Nerves Of. The ever popular Man Of." She paused. "Blue."

Kurt's grin turned into a full belly laugh. He'd forgotten how much fun she could be. "Unfortunately, they went with my mom's maiden name."

"Which was?"

"Strong."

"They didn't."

"Yep."

"Oh, my God," she managed, gasping. "Your name is Kurt Strong Steele?"

"It's on my birth certificate."

She giggled.

His heart swelled. She was a danger to his sanity, but a reckless part of him didn't care. "What's *your* middle name?" he asked.

"Nope."

"That's a weird one."

"I mean I'm not sharing, you dope."

"No fair."

"Who said I play fair?" she asked, her voice teasing at first, but fading at the end.

Of course his mind went immediately back to the sucker punch of finding out she'd been with another man while he was at training.

Maybe hers had too, because the line turned silent.

"Caitlyn?"

"It's Amelia."

"Seriously? As in Earhart?"

"I wish." She sighed. "No, as in Bedelia."

"*Who?*"

"My mom liked this children's book series about a woman named Amelia Bedelia when she was a kid. My dad thought it was too weird for a first name, so they compromised."

"Well, it beats Strong Steele. And you can always pretend you were presciently named after the pilot. Preferably without the disappearing part."

"Sure. We're making up stories anyway, right?"

"Exactly." And he'd do well to remember it.

What's your favorite color?

Caitlyn smiled to herself as she typed the text message from the comfort of the deserted general aviation terminal at Hewanorra on St. Lucia. Her client wouldn't return from her meeting for another hour, and Caitlyn had time to burn.

She and Kurt had been talking daily since she returned home, mostly to get their stories straight and ensure they knew the important details about each other. But, she might as well learn the little things about him too. Plus, it would drive him nuts.

Seriously?

His reply came almost instantly, despite the fact that it was nine a.m. on a Tuesday and he was probably at work, drumming up new clients, or assigning jobs, or reading through a contract. Maybe she was interrupting a meeting. But then, he could just ignore her.

She waited without responding and could imagine him sitting at his desk, drinking coffee—did he like it with cream and sugar, or black?—wearing those sexy reading glasses. Heat curled through her chest and spread to her fingers and toes. *Shake it off.* They weren't going there except to pretend.

Taking a sip of her Ju-C cola—a morning indulgence that made her neighbor Jade gag—she stroked Rockley's fur with one hand and turned her attention back to her e-reader, but the thriller from an author she usually liked failed to thrill her this morning.

Her phone buzzed.

Puce.

Caitlyn laughed out loud. Good thing there was no one around. And that she'd already swallowed her soda.

Bullshit.

He replied with the grinning emoticon.

Blue. You?

No, I'm feeling good today.

He sent her an eye roll.

She could imagine him shaking his head, amusement lighting up his handsome face. Jesus. She needed to stop this train of thought. She tapped on her phone's screen.

`Blue-green. Can't choose.`

`No fair.`

Three dots appeared to show he was typing again.

`You *have* to choose.`

She may have started this, but she hated picking favorites. Favorite movie, book, food. It was always changing. How did a person pick one and never change their mind?

`Turquoise.`

`Chicken.`

She laughed again, ignoring the stately white-haired man who entered the lounge and gave her a curious look.

`Favorite number.`

`19.`

`Double digits??`

Who picked a number that high?

`Go big or go home.`

`Mine's 5.`

She liked its shape for some reason. Always had.

`That's odd.`

She chuckled as she sent him a goofy face icon. Let the other pilot in the room wonder.

`You really think someone's going to ask us these?`

His deep voice echoed in her head as if he'd spoken the words out loud. She'd thought texting would be "safer" than calling, because his sexy voice twisted up her insides and turned her legs to wet noodles, but if she could conjure him speaking in her mind, no form of communication was safe.

What the hell was wrong with her?

She shook her head. They were friends. Maybe not even that. Her choice.

And probably his too, these days.

She tapped out a response.

You never know.

Doubtful, but she enjoyed provoking him. Until their relationship had gone sideways, it had been built largely on teasing and taunting. Turned out, she had missed that over the years.

Fine. This is relevant. Why do I always have to go to DC when we "meet up?"

For their story, it made sense to stick as close to the truth as possible in case Glenn went overboard and started looking into their travel histories. Kurt had never been to Barbados, whereas she had flown to the States at least once a year to visit Terrell and to see how being "home" felt. So far, she'd always wanted to return to Barbados.

He didn't answer for five minutes. She stared out the window at the lush green beyond the airport perimeter. Would they continue like this after he helped her rescue Rose? Could he forgive her and go back to being friends?

Her phone vibrated on her thigh.

I don't like to fly.

As if anyone would believe the big, tough former PJ who used to jump out of planes would be afraid of anything. Though, he had crashed... But he'd also agreed to come to the Caribbean for the party, so it couldn't be that.

How do we explain you being engaged to a pilot?

TSA is annoying when you're an amp.

Ah. She'd never thought about what it must be like to go through security now that he was disabled. He probably had to get the wand and the intrusive pat-down every time.

:-(So you're marrying me for free charter service.

He replied instantly.

Why else?

Her smile dropped. He was being sarcastic. She got that, but this whole situation was messing with her. She didn't want a boyfriend, or fiancé, or husband, but she still had a useless ego that took that hit hard.

What do I get out of the deal?

The glory that is me. Obviously.

She smiled, but Christ. She needed to knock some sense into the parts of her body that thought this was foreplay.

I assume you mean your bank account and your biceps.

You like my biceps?

Who wouldn't?

Because, honestly, they were palpitation-worthy.

What about me? I mean, besides owning a plane.

Fishing for compliments was unseemly. She deserved a smart-ass response.

Your freckles.

And there it was. Maybe he'd forgotten how sensitive she was about the splatter of brown that covered her from head to toe. She could have handled a few on her nose—those girls were "cute"—but her body had gone all in, and the kids in school had teased her mercilessly about it. They had called her Leopard or Spot, and chased her with a marker threatening to "connect the dots." She couldn't count the number of times some well-meaning person had told her she had chocolate on her lip.

Jerk.

Okay, um…

She waited. Was it really that hard for him to think of something nice to say?

Another message appeared on her phone's screen.

Your eyes. They're like polished emeralds lit with fire.

Her heart kicked. *Good God, now he was a poet.* But he was toying with her. *Wasn't he?* It was the only option she could handle.

`Bravo. You can rake muck with the best of them.`

The three dots appeared and then stopped several times.

Ten minutes passed.

Finally, he replied.

`Sorry, gotta go. I'll call later.`

Her body drooped. *How could she miss him already?* She tapped the thumbs-up response and stuck her phone in her pocket.

Maybe she and Kurt *couldn't* be friends after they rescued Rose. She might too easily come to rely on his presence in her life again, and that was a risk she couldn't take.

CHAPTER FIVE

KURT HAD ONCE LOVED FLYING. Since the crash, it had featured near the top of his list of activities to avoid, alongside drinking too much tequila and watching fishing on television.

He distracted himself on the flight from DC to Barbados by reviewing his notes on everything he and Caitlyn had covered in the two weeks since her unexpected visit had turned his life on its ear.

After crafting the story of how they'd met and coming up with a few other get-togethers in the farce of their long-distance love affair, they had—thank you, Jesus—moved on to safer topics. How she'd named her dog after the beach near where she'd found him. Her day-to-day life as a pilot. How much they both enjoyed being their own boss. The routine of Kurt's life running Steele, which gave him a sense of purpose and let him reclaim the brotherhood he'd had as a PJ.

Now, as the plane started its descent into Grantley Adams, he forced himself to breathe deeply on approach, and watched out the window so he could anticipate touchdown. The plane hit hard and bounced once, and he practically tore the armrests from the seat, but they made it.

Thank God the newlyweds next to him had slept for the entire flight and left him alone. There was nothing worse than having a neighboring passenger comment on his white-knuckle approach to flying.

How ironic that Caitlyn was a pilot. From the outside they seemed incompatible.

But he'd never thought so. Twelve years ago, he'd thought she was perfect for him. Smart, tough, gorgeous. He'd never met anyone like her.

But it had been the height of idiocy to expect a kiss to become something more, especially when he was poised to enter nearly two years of training—assuming he didn't wash out of Indoc, which eighty percent of guys did—followed by a high ops tempo of deployments for the next fifteen-or-so years. What kind of woman in her right mind would sign up for a relationship with a man who would never be home?

If she'd just *said* that, he might still be fantasizing about her, but he wouldn't have hated himself for it. It was the betrayal that had gutted him. But then, they hadn't made any promises. He'd merely made assumptions, formed expectations. He should have known better.

In his teen years, after one of many fights with his sister, Kurt's mom had told them, "Our anger isn't always as righteous as we think it is. We get mad when people—or life's events—don't meet our expectations. That doesn't necessarily mean they did something wrong or bad. It's just not what *you* wanted. And often, you end up hurting yourself more than them in the long run." He hadn't fully understood at the time. Only after she was gone did he realize how wise she'd been.

While catching up during the last two weeks, he and

Caitlyn had fallen back into their easy friendship, and just like before, he wanted more. Part of him recoiled at the idea, but did it really make sense to blame her for something that happened so long ago? They'd been kids. He didn't know why she'd kissed him and then hooked up with another man while he was gone, but it had been Kurt's fault for turning a single —admittedly hot—kiss into a promise of some kind. One he'd never asked for and she hadn't given.

Trusting her again wouldn't come easy, but dammit, he liked the woman she was now as much—maybe more than— the woman she'd been at twenty-two. And she seemed to like him too. Sure, he might be misreading her again. This trip was his chance to find out. Worst case, he was back where he started, but at least he would have tried. He could leave Barbados without regrets and move on.

In the back of his mind, without fully realizing it, he'd been using her as the gold standard for every woman he met. It wasn't fair to them or to him, because no one could ever be her. Even Caitlyn in the flesh wasn't the ideal of a woman that he had fashioned around her in his mind. But she was close enough to screw with him. And in many ways, better than some fantasy version.

He had two days with Caitlyn to show her how good they could be together, and he planned to make the most of them.

He shuffled off the plane and carefully navigated the roll-up stairs to the tarmac behind the other passengers, his shirt already stuck to his back with sweat. Customs and immigration awaited, but at least he wouldn't suffer scrutiny from security again. Flying as an amputee wasn't exactly a picnic these days.

Twenty minutes later, he found Caitlyn near the baggage claim area wearing a white tank top and tan shorts that showed off her long, athletic legs and a riot of dark freckles on pale skin.

He longed to connect all the dots. With his tongue.

She met him halfway with a solid hug that brought their bodies in contact from shoulders to hips. He held on tight as he imagined a man might who hadn't seen his fiancée for weeks. The way he'd wanted to hold her for years. She was lean but soft in his arms, and something in him eased as he held her. Maybe it was her fresh, outdoorsy scent or her smooth skin. Whatever it was, embracing her was "right" in a way it could never be with another woman. If he hadn't been sure she was worth a second chance before, he was now.

She pulled away to give him a quick cinnamon-gum flavored kiss on the lips that brought back a flood of memories, and then smiled. "I missed you."

So the show starts now.

His insides went haywire. "Me too, hon." He smoothed back a loose strand of her hair, prolonging contact. "You look great."

Her cheeks flushed. She gave him another too-short kiss and grabbed his hand.

He ignored the stares and surreptitious looks as they moved through the crowd toward the exit. Six years in, he was used to it. When he could first walk on his prosthetic legs, he'd worn pants everywhere. Now he didn't give a shit. He'd rather be comfortable than worry about making others comfortable with his appearance. In fact, outside of work, he often wore shorts well into winter.

Within ten minutes, they sat in her old Land Rover motoring down the left side of the road past grass and fields of some crop, palm trees, and lush stands of trees that rivaled anything in Virginia. They were flanked by green jungle on the hills to their left, and gorgeous blue ocean out the driver's side window. "I can see the appeal, but is it warm and humid all year long?" he asked.

"I seem to recall you thinking this would be the perfect weather once upon a time."

"Yeah, well, I run hot now."

She gave him an uncertain look, maybe trying to decide if he was messing with her. "I don't think anybody's bugged my car," she said. "We can relax in here."

"That wasn't an innuendo." But it could've been. God knew just the sight of her raised his temperature. "Amputees have less surface area to release heat, and walking on prosthetic legs takes far more energy than walking on my own legs did." On the plus side, winter in DC no longer sucked.

"Oh." She frowned slightly, and her eyes scanned from the road to her mirrors, and back again.

"Everything okay?" he asked.

"Yeah." She tucked a long piece of hair that had fallen from her braid behind one ear. "Just checking for a tail."

"You think you're being followed?" He glanced in the side mirror.

She adjusted her grip on the steering wheel. "I don't know. One of the men I helped rescue last month was found beaten and left for dead last night in Vieux Fort. On St. Lucia. Police are calling it a mugging gone wrong, but if he was tortured for information—"

"He might have described you."

"He might. I'm probably just being paranoid about that one, but Glenn has been increasingly aggressive the last couple of weeks. At this point, I wouldn't put anything past him." Her fake engagement ring caught the sunlight and sent tiny white sparkles across the interior of the car.

"This guy's starting to sound more like a stalker." Why hadn't she mentioned any of this on the phone?

"I'm honestly not sure. I take Rockley with me when I fly,

so he's not home to guard my house when I'm away. There have been a couple of times lately when I thought maybe someone had been inside, but I couldn't find anything definitive. No signs of a break-in, nothing taken or obviously moved."

"Jesus, Cait. Have you thought about installing cameras or security? Or checking for bugs?"

"This guy I know, a former Navy SEAL who teaches dive classes here, came and checked for bugs and installed a nanny cam. He didn't find anything."

A guy she knows. A former Navy SEAL. "Why didn't you ask the SEAL to pose as your fiancé?" He couldn't keep the barb out of his voice.

She glanced at him. "It's not like that. I don't know him very well. We have overlapping clients sometimes is all. Besides," she licked her lips, "I don't hunt where I live."

Kurt scowled and watched the jungle pass by out his window. He had no right, but he didn't like to think about her "hunting" at all.

Twenty minutes later she parked in front of a small yellow house with a green roof and shutters and a short, white picket fence around the front yard. They stepped out into the warm sun. "It's small, but I love it. The beach is about a quarter-mile that way, and I'm pretty close to the airport. The perfect setup."

"You really did it," he said, unable to keep some of the awe out of his voice.

She met him at the back of the SUV. "What's that?"

"Your dream." He removed his duffel bag and followed her through a small gate to the front door, which was covered in louvers. Muffled barking came from inside the house. "Becoming a pilot, starting your own charter business in the Caribbean, having a house near the ocean." She had managed it all.

Not that he would complain about his own circumstances. He'd lived his dream of being a PJ for four years. That was more than most people ever got. And life was still good.

She unlocked the door and looked over her shoulder with a smile. "Yeah. I guess I did."

About fifty pounds of scruffy black dog quivered just beyond the threshold, eyeing Kurt warily even as his tail wagged with enthusiasm.

"This is Rockley," Caitlyn said. "Ro, this is Kurt. He's a friend."

Rockley barked once and then approached Kurt tentatively, sniffing the hand he held out.

"Hey, buddy," Kurt said. "Do you smell Max?"

"He doesn't always like white men, but he seems to think you're okay."

Kurt petted the dog's head and scratched behind his ears. "We're not all bastards." What kind of sicko would beat a dog? "He looks happy and healthy now. You've obviously been good for him."

"*He's* been good for *me*." She smiled. "He's easy to love."

"I'm sure." Kurt refused to be jealous of a dog.

He straightened, an elephant in a dollhouse in the low-ceilinged house that had only one exit. Despite its size and lack of egress options, the living room to his left was inviting, with a love seat and chair upholstered in light brown and the color of shallow water on the walls. Several small paintings of island scenes adorned the spaces between jalousie windows. A window air conditioner pumped out welcome cool air.

"This is nice," he said. "Like a vacation getaway."

She looked around with a satisfied expression. "Thanks. These don't come up for sale very often. I got lucky." Waving toward the rear, left corner of the house, she said, "Kitchen, obviously. The bathroom is through that door." She pointed to a narrow doorway across from the kitchen.

Her place was definitely not disabled friendly, but then most homes weren't.

The kitchen overlooked the side yard where a riot of pink and yellow blooms reached for the window. Beyond her small garden were other colorful little homes and the occasional palm tree swaying in the breeze. He could see the appeal.

"You can put your bag in here," Caitlyn said as Rockley followed them through into a room to the right that was just big enough to fit a queen bed and a dresser. A silky quilt in tones of blue and green contrasted with the pale orange walls that gave the room a vibrant energy.

"Sorry, it's not puce."

He laughed. A welcome release. "I wouldn't know it if I saw it."

"Shocker," she said with raised eyebrows, her eyes glinting with mischief. "So, feel free to take a nap or whatever. If you need a snack, help yourself to anything in the kitchen." She opened the top dresser drawer. "I cleared this one out for you." Turning, she gestured to a doorway covered by a curtain embroidered in large flowers. "There are a few empty hangers in the closet."

"Thanks." One bedroom. It wasn't exactly like he could stay in a nearby hotel if they wanted anyone to believe they were romantically involved. But taking over one of her drawers and hanging his clothes in her closet was oddly intimate, and jarring.

"Is the sofa a pullout?" If not, it was far too small for either of them. Maybe she had an air mattress. He'd assumed she had the sleeping arrangements figured out, and he hadn't been able to bring himself to broach the topic.

"Yes." She cleared her throat. "But I figure it's too short for you, so you can have my bed while you're here."

Holy hell. Sleeping in Caitlyn's bed had once been the stuff of his fantasies. With her in it, of course. Could he turn the dream into a reality, with her right next to him, under him, over him? Hell, any way she wanted him.

If not, for the next few days, he'd be driving himself a little bit mad playing house with her, holding and kissing her, and knowing the entire time it was all a lie.

Glenn Lambert sat on the beach behind his family's plantation house on St. Isidore, his latest arm candy on a lounger next to him.

Not the woman he really wanted. She didn't have dark red hair, or masses of freckles, or that compelling cloak of self-assurance that Caitlyn carried. Part of him simply craved a taste of that feeling, part of him wanted to knock her down a peg.

She thought she was too good for him?

Even more perplexing was that she'd chosen a muscle-bound invalid over him. Why would a woman who could have a wealthy, powerful, handsome man like Glenn want to be with a guy like that? Not that she and Steele were together much, despite their recent engagement.

Maybe that was part of his appeal.

Glenn had begun to suspect that she'd made up the fiancé until he did some digging. The man's job in security made him uncomfortable, but Steele wasn't law enforcement, and everything checked out as legit. Plus, the man was an amputee, so how much of a threat could he be?

Still, Glenn had sent Lawrence to follow them. If there was even the slightest chance that she was lying about this guy, he wanted to know about it. There was too much at stake to let her get close to the family if she couldn't be trusted. He couldn't help feeling that she was a threat. One he wanted to fuck, but still...

Rumor had it that the pilot who had been flying for The Underground recently was a white woman. There were several female pilots in the islands, and those were just the ones who worked as such. There could be any number of amateurs willing to help The Underground. But Caitlyn was the only outsider close enough to Glenn's family to learn more about Island Profiles Incorporated—IPI—the enterprise his father had started decades ago. As much as he didn't want to believe she would betray them, he hadn't been able to rule her out.

"Glenn, we have to clear the beach so the crew can set up," Arielle called from behind him. "And lunch is ready."

"I'll be up to the house in a minute." He waved off his sister and stood. "Elena?" The curvy blonde removed her shades and smiled at him. "You ready?" he asked.

She rose gracefully from the chair, the tiny white bikini she wore accentuating her curves and leaving little to the imagination. "Always."

His dad would not approve, which made her perfect. Glenn had very few ways to assert his independence from his father without being disowned. But that would change soon enough. Things hadn't been going to plan, but Glenn had a new scheme in the works.

He was done waiting for his father's approval to turn the business into something bigger than his dad had ever envisioned. Done waiting to claim what was his. His father would soon see how badly he'd underestimated his only son.

"Sir!" Lawrence strode across the sand, his coconut brown skin glistening with sweat.

Glenn turned to Elena. "Cocktail dress. I'll pick you up at

five-thirty."

She lowered her eyelids and gave him a coy look, as if she were shy, but he knew better. She grabbed her phone and drink and sashayed toward the house, hips swinging enticingly.

"What is it?" he asked Lawrence.

"I followed them like you asked. She picked him up and then drove straight to her house. They were still there when I left."

"Did they look," he waved his hand vaguely, "in love?"

Lawrence shrugged. "Mussy." *Maybe.* "They kissed."

Black edged Glenn's vision. He shouldn't have asked. "What about the other thing we were working on?"

"He said that the pilot was a white woman. It was dark and she wore a hat, and he was too scared to notice more. I've tracked down two more. Bhodi and I are going to 'speak' with them this evening."

"Good. But this time, make sure they can't wake up to tell tales."

Lawrence nodded repeatedly. "Yes, sir. Bhodi's taking care of that problem now, and we'll be more...thorough with these two."

"Excellent." Glenn rubbed his hands together. Bringing down The Underground would ensure IPI could continue to grow unfettered. And Glenn had ideas that would drive it to new heights. "Ten thousand for each of you if you identify the pilot before tonight's party."

CHAPTER SIX

TWO HOURS AFTER CAITLYN MANAGED to refrain from tackling Kurt into her bed, they sat at her small table eating a platter of cut fruit. God, the look he'd given her when they discussed sleeping arrangements… She'd been tempted to stick her head in the freezer by the time she left the room.

He'd always been tempting, but she'd somehow managed to keep those feelings under lock and key around him. Well, except for that ill-advised kiss that ruined everything. But now, it was as if he'd taken a sledgehammer to the vault where she'd sequestered her desire and everything came pouring out, exciting and messy and unwelcome.

Kurt tapped her hand and she jumped. "Hey," he said. "You okay?"

"Yeah. Just thinking about Rose." As she should have been.

He covered her fingers with his warm hand. "We'll get her."

Caitlyn nodded and reluctantly slid her hand free.

"You know, if you're going to be this jumpy around me at

the party, no one will believe we're really a couple."

"Sorry. I'll focus." She couldn't risk Glenn or Treavor Lambert seeing through their ruse. Rose's life depended on it. Somehow she needed to relax and enjoy being with Kurt without losing herself to him.

"You shouldn't have to. Being together needs to be easy. Second nature."

She nodded.

"Maybe we should practice." His suggestive grin had her swallowing hard.

"Practice, huh?" She slid her hand up his wrist, the hair on his muscular forearms soft against her fingertips. "Like this?"

His dark eyes gleamed as his smiled faded. "That's a good start." Raising his free hand, he stroked his thumb across her cheekbone.

It took all of her willpower to hold his gaze as his fingers slid behind her ear and down the sensitive skin of her neck. A shiver ran through her as he glanced at her lips and cupped the back of her head. Why couldn't she just give in? For Rose. Maybe even for herself.

Kurt watched her, color rising in his cheeks as he leaned infinitesimally closer. She inhaled his subtle masculine scent and closed her eyes, narrowing the gap between them until her mouth unerringly found his, as inevitable and unavoidable as the nearby waves caressing the shore. His hot, soft lips pressed to hers, soothing, seeking, capturing.

He licked the outline of her upper lip and she gasped at the sparks that skated through her stomach. Rather than take advantage, he waited, pressing soft kisses to her mouth, tasting her lips until she finally broke and sought his tongue with her own. First contact sent a jolt through her body, and the room was suddenly sweltering. He tasted like pineapple and sex and something inexplicable and addictive. She wanted to crawl into his lap and—

Kurt broke the kiss, his breath coming fast and his dark eyes sparkling as he smiled. "That's more like it." He planted a quick kiss on her nose and straightened, releasing her and pulling free. "Act more like that and we'll be fine tonight."

What?

Pulling free of her grip, Kurt excused himself from the tiny cafe table and carried his plate into the kitchen with Rockley on his heels, as if they hadn't just shared the hottest kiss she'd had since she gave in to her curiosity twelve years ago.

Caitlyn forced herself to stop staring. How did he go from devouring her one minute to acting like they'd shared nothing but polite conversation the next?

"I should probably change if we're going to leave soon," he said, looking good enough to eat in a black T-shirt and tan cargo shorts.

In Caitlyn's memories, Kurt had muscled thighs and calves covered in dark hair, so the sight of his artificial legs was momentarily jarring. But women were probably as attracted to him now as they had been when she, Kurt, and Terrell had gone barhopping in OKC. Maybe more. His youthful arrogance had been replaced with a solemn confidence born of hardships and horrors she could only imagine.

"Will this interfere with our flight?" he asked, jerking his chin at the ceiling. Rain beat a steady rhythm overhead, dripping from the sloped roof and splattering the windows.

Shaking her head to clear the fog in her brain, she said, "I doubt it. Showers rarely last long around here."

"Mm." He almost sounded disappointed.

The muscles in his forearms rippled as he dried his plate,

and she had to look away. Good grief. She needed to get a grip. She could not get involved with Kurt. On the rare occasions she got laid, she sought out a man she could guarantee she'd never see or do business with again. One who wouldn't try to lay claim to her or start a relationship.

She wanted to see Kurt again after this week, and sex would complicate things. *Not worth it*. Hell, she didn't even know the extent of his injuries. Maybe he couldn't…

But damn if he didn't smell delicious.

She cleared her throat. "You want the bathroom or the bedroom first?"

"Before I get cleaned up, do you have any pictures of Rose? I'd like to know who to look for."

He came around to the table as she thumbed through photos on her phone and then held it out to him, trying to keep enough distance between them to avoid his magnetic pull.

"Is that her natural hair color?" he asked about her sister's mass of tight, coppery curls.

"Yeah. She gets that a lot." Rose's hair was as dark red as Caitlyn's, despite her golden brown skin. "Her dad must carry the recessive redhead gene, which my mom obviously has too. It's not common, but there's a photographer who's documenting mixed-race redheads from all over the world. Rose was amazed to see other people like her with red hair and brown skin. My brother, on the other hand, takes after his dad, brown hair, brown eyes, no freckles, maybe a shade lighter."

Caitlyn shared several more photos of Rose, but she was pretty easy to spot in a crowd. "I was three years ahead of her in school, but we bonded over being freckled redheads. Especially when some of the kids started bullying her for her appearance. Strawberry Shortcake, etc. She had it far worse than I did—like kids asking, 'What are you?'—but she seemed to handle it better."

Kurt frowned. "Kids suck sometimes." He returned the phone. "Actually, so do some adults."

Caitlyn could only nod as a deep ache invaded her chest. Why had she let her relationship with her sister languish? What if she and Kurt couldn't save Rose? Caitlyn pressed a hand to her knotted stomach, now wishing she hadn't eaten.

"You okay?" Kurt asked, touching her shoulder lightly and far too briefly.

Shoving aside the fear and regret, she straightened and pushed away from the table. "I'm fine. Thanks." There was no room, no time, for emotions.

Within an hour, the skies had cleared, and they were on their way to St. Isidore in her Piper Navajo. She rarely wore her hair down, and she was already regretting it as sweat formed on the back of her neck and strands of hair caught in the headset, tugging at her scalp.

"Do you get airsick?" she asked through the microphone.

Kurt sat pale and silent next to her in a charcoal suit and gray button-down shirt with the collar open. "No. I just don't enjoy flying much these days."

"Since Afghanistan?" Since his helicopter had crashed and he'd nearly died.

"Yeah."

Shit. He hadn't been kidding when he said he didn't like to fly. She'd had no idea how much she was asking when she begged him to come here. "Why didn't you say something? We could have rented a boat."

He glanced at her. "I'm fine. Better to face it down."

And that was so like him. Not fearless—because who really was?—but brave. Always pushing his limits. Testing himself. Never giving himself an inch of leeway when it came to the hard stuff. She'd allowed herself to forget some of his best qualities after their friendship had fallen apart.

They flew over the crystal turquoise waters of the Caribbean in relative silence, the only sound the purr of the propellers. Caitlyn lived for this. The sky was freedom. Freedom from the expectations and limitations put on her by society, from the pressure to be "feminine," to get married and have children, to measure her self-worth by her appearance or pedigree.

Not to mention, it was flat-out exhilarating to cheat gravity. Her little Piper might not be an F-16, but it got her in the air. Up here, the world was small. Insignificant. Nothing mattered but staying aloft.

All too quickly, they were skirting St. Isidore's southern coastline. Less than thirty miles long, the island had a rough arrowhead shape, with a mountain and rainforest on the southwestern end of the wide base, and dense jungle covering the rural areas. Lambert's plantation sat on the coast, in a valley just north of Montagne de St. Pierre, a mountain that rose straight out of the Caribbean Sea.

"That's it?" Kurt asked, his gaze out the window.

"Uh-huh."

"The guys weren't exaggerating when they said it was beautiful. Too bad it's such a shit show."

"Yeah. Things are getting better, but there's a lot of work to do. Your team has had a positive impact here. You can be proud of that."

"I guess so." They rounded the lush mountain and dropped altitude. "Other than Tara, I'm the only one who's never been here. Hell, even Mick was here as a PJ on a humanitarian mission."

"Mick?"

Kurt glanced at her. "One of my old teammates. The one

who kept me alive after the crash."

Thank you, Mick, whoever you are.

"I thought he was going to join me at Steele," Kurt said, "but he got married. To Tara's best friend actually, which is how I met *her*. Mick and Jenna moved to South Carolina a few years ago, and now have a little boy. Robby's two."

Something in his voice made her ask, "Do you want kids?"

"I love my nephew, and I think having my own children would be great, but finding the right woman is more important. Kids would be a bonus, but I'm not exactly getting younger."

Her chest tightened at the wistful look on his face. He'd be a great dad. Solid, steady, playful, fair. Present. "What are you talking about? You have plenty of time. Men can make babies into their seventies. Just look at that actor…James whatever. The one in that new movie about World War II."

"Rockaway?"

"Right."

"Sure, it's possible, but if I have kids, I don't want to be too old to play with them. Obviously, there are no guarantees, but I'd like to be around to see them grow up, maybe to be a grandpa."

Her heart twisted. Even if she let herself be with Kurt, she couldn't give him the family he really wanted. "I can see it now, Papa Steele. You'd spoil those kids rotten."

"Absolutely." He laughed. "It's in the job description."

For his sake, she hoped he got the job.

For the first time since his crash, flying wasn't so bad. Being stuck next to Caitlyn in close quarters helped. She smelled fresh as sunshine and rain, and shone bright as a jewel in a green dress that showcased her athletic shoulders and shapely legs. And an endless landscape of fascinating freckles.

He hadn't meant for things to go as far as they had this afternoon. He was trying to move slowly, trying not to scare her away. He'd thought maybe a few caresses, maybe a gentle kiss, would remind her how good they were together. Get her thinking about the possibilities. *And* be more comfortable for their mission. But holy combustion, she had lit him up. He'd had to pull away before he let things go too far and sent her running for the hills.

Now, Caitlyn had stopped talking as she prepared for landing, and Kurt turned his attention to the beauty *outside* his window. The plane turned away from the evening sun and descended toward St. Isidore, where Dan and Mick had once spent three weeks providing medical care and aid to earthquake victims. Where Dan had first met his wife Alyssa, a nurse for a non-profit, six years ago, and reconnected with her again three years later.

At least now Kurt could put a place to their stories.

He managed not to bruise the armrests as Caitlyn brought the plane in low along a wide valley nestled in the foothills of the mountain that towered over the lush island.

She took a long arc around a sprawling home ringed by grass, thick bushes, and palms. Rows of banana plants and trees with fat leaves filled several acres surrounding the paved runway that seemed to appear at the last minute.

The touchdown was so smooth, they might as well have been riding a feather onto a pillow. A perfect, three-point landing. "Wow. Dan wasn't kidding."

"About what?" she asked, slowing the plane on the short runway.

"Your skills as a pilot."

"Thanks." She grinned. "Why do you think I get the big bucks?" Her pink cheeks belied her flippant response, but he didn't doubt that clients appreciated her expertise. Or her smile.

Once the plane stopped and she had shut down the engines, several men approached the plane, armed with AKs.

"We're expected, right?"

She unfastened her harness and removed her headset, shaking out her silky hair. "Yes. And I know these guys."

God, she was even more of a distraction than usual. Not good now that he needed to keep his wits about him. "I know you said they'd check for weapons, but I don't like going unarmed." The only "insurance" they'd brought was a wad of cash. He freed himself from his seat and ran a hand through his hair to remove any marks left by the headset.

"It'll be fine. Trust me." Easing her way to the back, she opened the hatch.

"It's not you I have issues with."

"Hey, guys," she said to the guards with a wave. "Would you mind putting the chocks down? I don't want to get anything on my dress."

"Yes, ma'am." A thick arm reached for the blocks and disappeared.

Caitlyn kicked off the running shoes and socks she'd worn for flying and slipped on short, strappy, black heels that would bring her nearly eye-to-eye with him. "Ready?" she asked, waving him closer.

"As I'll ever be." He descended the narrow stairs slowly, following her into the soft air.

"We need to check the plane, Ms. Brevard," said a barrel-chested white man with a permanently sunburned nose and an Aussie accent.

"Standard procedure," she murmured to Kurt as she waved the man inside. "Go ahead, Jack."

He returned a minute later. "All clear."

The men gave Kurt and Caitlyn a cursory pat down and checked her purse, and finally waved them on. It looked like they weren't taking any chances with security after the attempt on Lambert's life a few weeks back. Even with the woman who'd saved him.

When the guards returned to their posts around the perimeter of the airfield, Caitlyn closed the hatch. She took Kurt's hand and they strolled toward the plantation's back gate. Golden sun backlit the house, making it impossible to make out the home's features, and casting the runway in shadow.

A cool breeze made the warm, sticky air nearly bearable in his jacket. Thank God he didn't have to wear a tie too.

Leaning toward Caitlyn, he got a lungful of her enticing scent. "You look amazing."

"Thanks." She smiled and gave him a quick kiss on the lips that left him reeling.

Up ahead, the wrought-iron-and-wood gate swung open and a man in his late twenties with light brown hair and a smug smile blocked their path. "Caitlyn." His lecherous gaze traveled down her body and back up again. "Wow. You look fabulous."

Who the hell was this punk? They'd just arrived, but was it too soon to punch someone?

"Thanks." Caitlyn squeezed Kurt's hand. She probably wanted to sock the asshole too. "I'd like you to meet my fiancé Kurt Steele." She turned to Kurt. "This is Glenn Lambert. Treavor Lambert's son."

"Hi, there," Kurt said as he stuck out his right hand. He couldn't bring himself to tell the man he was pleased to meet him.

He was prepared for some kind of power play, but Glenn gave him a quick, firm handshake and stepped out of their way with his arm out toward the house. "Enjoy the party. I'm sure I'll see you around."

"Okay." Caitlyn shivered and tugged Kurt up the brick path. When they were out of earshot, she said, "He makes my skin crawl."

Kurt rubbed the back of her hand with his thumb and glanced back to see Glenn watching them. "You have good instincts."

Lambert's house had been transformed. Small star-shaped lights hung in clusters from the wood beams that ran the length of the ceiling in a magical display. Dozens of round tables filled the great room, covered with turquoise or salmon tablecloths and large centerpieces of tropical flowers arrayed in a flat circle.

One would think this was the wedding reception.

Too bad Caitlyn couldn't enjoy it, even with the sexy man on her arm, though she liked having Kurt by her side far more than she'd expected. The look in Glenn's eyes when he greeted them at the back gate had been more predatory than usual. Darker somehow.

She shouldn't chafe at wanting backup. It wasn't a sign of weakness. Even special ops guys worked in teams.

"Any sign of her?" Kurt asked, his breath tickling her neck and raising goosebumps on her skin as he casually scanned the room.

Caterers filled the chafing dishes at the buffet, and servers circled the room with trays of drinks and appetizers. Reini, the woman of formidable size she'd met two weeks ago in the kitchen, stood in a corner dispatching a crew to clear tables and clean up mishaps.

None of them were Rose. For all Caitlyn knew, these were outside catering or legitimate hired help.

"No. Not yet."

He squeezed her hand. "We'll find her."

They played the happily engaged couple as the real engaged couple sat at one end of the room, flanked by their families. After dinner and a round of speeches from the fathers of the bride and groom, Lambert revealed a dance floor on the back lawn overlooking the beach. A string quartet played music, and couples filtered outside where another bar had been staged.

As she and Kurt rose from the table, Treavor Lambert approached.

"That's Lambert," she said under her breath.

"Ms. Brevard!" The man beamed at her so genuinely, she could almost forget he was a devil under the charming facade. "I'm so glad you made it. And this must be your lucky man."

"Yessir. Hi." Somehow, she managed to smile. "This is Kurt Steele," she said as the men shook hands.

"Nice to meet you, sir," Kurt said.

Lambert winked at him and gave them both a genial grin. "It's good to meet *you*. I was beginning to think the little lady here was blowing smoke just to keep Glenn away from her."

Caitlyn managed a breathy laugh.

Kurt slid his arm around her shoulder and pulled her tight to his side. The possessive move sent a little thrill clear to her toes. She might like her independence, but some part of her enjoyed a man who took charge. As long as he didn't take too much.

"We're still trying to sort out the logistics," Kurt said, "but we won't let a couple thousand miles keep us apart."

The older man's eyes twinkled. Unlike his son, Lambert's depravity didn't leak out from beneath his navy suit like a bitter fog. "She's definitely worth hanging onto, this one. But I'm hoping you don't steal her away too soon. Not only is she the best pilot I've ever flown with, this little woman saved my life. Did she tell you that?"

Little woman? Caitlyn managed not to wrinkle her nose. Amazing how he could be so condescending and complimentary in the same sentence. And, of course, he assumed she'd be the one giving up her life when they married.

"Yes, sir, she did." Kurt's big, warm hand squeezed her shoulder. "I gotta say, I'm not too excited about her getting shot at. I thought we left that behind in the Air Force." There was no mistaking the irritation in his voice. If she didn't know better she'd fully believe he was an aggrieved fiancé.

"You'll be glad to know, then, that I have doubled my security, especially patrols in the jungle and plantation."

Shit. Doubled?

Lambert shrugged and shook his head. "The more successful you become, the more people want to take you down." He said it like a man with nothing to hide. Like a man who didn't mislead desperate people and use blackmail or threats to force them to work under horrible conditions.

She found it increasingly difficult to hide her distaste for the entire Lambert family in the weeks since she'd discovered Rose. And now she and Kurt had only a couple of hours to locate her sister and the others and get them out to the van waiting several streets over for her call. Sadly, not all of them would be willing to leave.

Fear was a powerful yoke.

"I can only imagine," Kurt said to Lambert, pulling Caitlyn's attention back to the conversation. "I guess everyone struggles."

"Indeed," Lambert said, with no trace of irony.

"I hope you don't mind if I whisk my date away for a dance in the moonlight. Your home is too beautiful not to take advantage of the moment."

"Not at all, young man." Lambert turned to her. "Ms. Brevard, thank you for joining my family for this happy occasion."

"Of course. Thank you for inviting us. We're honored to be here." She wanted to rinse out her mouth with bleach. If only she could go back to believing he was a wealthy-but-benign man who greased a few palms to get his business done. All the money she'd taken from him—was still taking, but now with a purpose—had been earned not just illegally, but immorally. "Enjoy your evening, and my congratulations again to your daughter and your family."

"Thank you."

Kurt whisked her through the back doors and carefully descended the steps to a large brick patio ringed by columns that stood like good soldiers ready for drill. "What an ass," he murmured.

Gauzy fabric had been draped around the perimeter, lit with small white lights and paper lanterns. Beyond the far columns, the lawn sloped down toward the sand, jungle on either side framing a view of the Caribbean Sea with a broad swatch of silver moonlight painting a path across the water.

Kurt gave a low whistle. "This place is incredible." The cool breeze ruffled his dark hair as he took her into his arms for a slow dance. His touch burned right through her dress.

"Built on the backs of slaves in the heyday of sugar plantations, and now maintained with the labor of modern-day slaves." She kept her voice low and her smile firmly in place. "Now that my blinders are off, I can hardly stand to be here."

He distracted her with small circles on her lower back. Only pride kept her from melting into his arms completely. "You're doing great," he said. "I had no idea what an accomplished actor you are."

She met his gaze, and it darkened when she combed her fingers into the short hair on the back of his neck. Was he acting now? Was she? In spite of their mission, the magical location combined with Kurt's arms around her waist made her feel a bit reckless. "I'm not that good," she said, tightness building in her chest.

Her gaze strayed to his lips.

He kissed her. A jolt of energy shot through her veins and she kissed back. Hard. The depth of her lust left her stunned. He was everything she feared.

She pulled away slowly with a shaky laugh. "Don't get too carried away, we're still in public."

His hold on her tightened, pressing her breasts to his solid chest. "I thought that was the whole point," he said, his deep, intimate voice a soft caress gliding over her skin.

She struggled to catch her breath with him looking at her like she was the next course in his favorite meal. And then she noticed Glenn on the dance floor with a beautiful blond woman.

Caitlyn's heart turned cold. She needed to find Rose and convince her to get out of this place before they lost their chance. Before she had to spend another hour here. "One more kiss and then we're going to wander away from here to be alone."

Kurt nodded. She touched her lips to his, and unable to resist, took a quick taste with her tongue. He moaned and deepened the kiss. In another life, under different circumstances, she'd maneuver him into the shadow of the trees and kiss him senseless.

With a sigh, she forced herself to disengage and glanced around. It wasn't wise to make a scene. But, luckily, nobody else was paying any attention to them.

Except Glenn. The slimy bastard stared daggers at her from ten yards away.

She blinked and let her gaze roam as if she hadn't noticed. Kurt loosened his hold, so she backed out of his arms and took his hand. "Care to take a stroll through the garden?" she asked.

"I'd love to."

They walked hand-in-hand at a leisurely pace through the expertly sculpted topiary, a contrast to the wild growth at the edge of the manicured grounds. As they rounded the corner to the south side of the villa, she checked to see if anyone was following them. Glenn was still on the brightly lit dance floor with his partner, but another couple talked quietly next to a column on the porch, and a guard with an AK-47 set a leisurely pace along the edge of the dark wilderness.

Keeping her voice low, Caitlyn said, "That should be the place." According to Shaylee's intel, the workers slept in the house to their right. The two-story servants' quarters mirrored the style of the great house with a much smaller footprint, maybe twenty-five hundred square feet total.

"Why don't we check out that fountain?" Kurt said in a normal tone, nudging her toward a vine-covered pergola that led to a stone fountain, partially hidden from the main house.

Caitlyn swung their joined hands and faced him. "A less trusting girl would think you were trying to get me alone so you could compromise me," she said, with what she hoped was a flirty smile that wasn't as hard to fake as it should have been.

"A less trusting girl would be right."

Oh my. She passed through the pergola and into the circular space created by trees that ringed the dry fountain. Kurt followed and sat on a cement bench, immediately tugging her sideways onto his lap. The hard frames of his prosthetic limbs caught her by surprise and she jolted. "Oh."

"Too uncomfortable?" he asked.

"No. I just…forgot."

"It's okay. I still do too, sometimes," he said, his weak smile barely visible in the shadows.

Unsure how to respond, she pressed her hands to his freshly shaved cheeks, holding his dark gaze as she pulled him in for a soft kiss. He held the back of her head and tattooed her mouth with whisper-light, breathy kisses that made her heart race.

"The guard went around the corner, and the couple moved inside," he said before gently sucking her lower lip into his mouth.

She ran her tongue across his upper lip.

With a groan, he took the kiss deeper, their tongues gliding sensuously as his warm hands slid up her ribcage. He kissed his way across her jaw and down the sensitive skin of her neck.

Oh, God. She pressed her aching breasts to his muscular chest, helpless under the soft, wet press of his lips and the gentle scrape of his teeth. He'd reduced her to an incendiary bundle of nerves ready to explode at his lightest touch.

What the hell were they doing? She dragged her fingers across the short, silky hair at the base of his neck and urged his head up. To soften her sudden withdrawal, she gave him a quick kiss on the lips and scanned the garden. "Looks safe now," she whispered, as if it had all been for show.

His chest rose and fell in time with hers. "Right." He sounded a little dazed as he loosened his hold and let her slide from his lap. While she straightened her dress, he sat motionless on the bench with his eyes closed, taking deep, measured breaths.

"You okay?" she asked.

"Never better." He slowly stood, rubbing his palm across his mouth, his amazing mouth that made her system go haywire. With a quick glance around, he stood and clasped her hand in his. "Let's do it."

Kurt released Caitlyn's hand and followed her along the narrow, shrub-lined path that led to the servant quarters. The only light came from the tree-filtered moon and a dim bulb over the front door of the two-story outbuilding with plantation shutters on every window.

Why the hell had he agreed to Caitlyn's scheme again? He could still taste her sweet, salty skin on his lips, still feel her soft curves under his palms and her breasts crushed against him. And, God help him, if he could, he'd stash her away and pick up where they'd left off.

Real life was far better than his dreams. How the hell was he supposed to go home and forget about her now? Only a fool would think he could be part of this ploy without getting hurt.

But then, he knew a little about surviving pain.

You'll live. Just get your head back in the game.

A fat raindrop splashed onto his nose, and within seconds, the sky opened up.

Caitlyn's pace picked up, but they were already drenched. His dress shoes slipped on the wet tiles, forcing him to tread carefully. The last thing he needed was to end up on his ass.

When they reached the narrow shelter of the porch, Kurt used his dripping-wet body to block her from view of the main house while she tried the door handle.

"It's locked," she mouthed. Her wet hair stuck to her face and lay in clumps on her shoulders. Water droplets fell from her nose. She was beautiful, even soaked and bedraggled, her dress glued to her body.

Dragging away his gaze, he examined the lock, then pulled a slim set of picks from his wallet. The guards hadn't thought to look there. "Keep an eye out."

With a nod, she turned her back on him. His hands were slippery, he hadn't practiced in months, and Caitlyn stood too close for him to ignore, but he managed to conquer the lock in under a minute.

"We're in," he said, dropping the tools into his pocket and pushing open the wooden door.

"All clear out here." She slid past him into the dimly lit foyer, waiting for him to close the door behind them before advancing down the hall.

They dripped and squished, leaving behind a trail of water on the carpet runner that muffled their approach to the central staircase. A quick circuit of the lower floor revealed a kitchen, a lounge, and a large dining room.

The rain pounded on the roof overhead, drowning out all other noise as they circled back to the foyer.

"Don't move." Glenn stepped into the anteroom holding a Glock, his wet hair dripping onto the floor.

Kurt froze, shielding Caitlyn with his body. Why hadn't he found a way to sneak in a weapon?

"Glenn, put the gun down," the damn foolish woman said, stepping out of his shadow and into the line of fire. "It's just us."

A black man dressed in a T-shirt and jeans stood behind Glenn, pointing a Sig Sauer at Kurt's chest.

"I can see that," Glenn said. "What are you doing in here?"

"I could ask you the same thing." Caitlyn stepped closer, pushing Kurt's blood pressure up another notch. "We were looking for shelter from the downpour and this was closer than the main house. You?"

Richie Rich looked skeptical. "Shelter? Or a bed?"

Even if he was insanely jealous, the guns seemed like overkill. What had they walked into?

She made a face. "Don't be crude. We just wanted someplace warm and dry to wait out the rain."

"So you broke in? You must think I'm an idiot."

Hands on hips, she said, "No, but I thought you trusted me by now. Your dad does. I saved his life, remember?"

Glenn's gaze raked her body from head to toe. "That *was* unfortunate."

She stared, eyes wide. "What do you mean?"

He shrugged. "Patience has never been my strong suit."

What the fuck? Had the guy really admitted to an attempt on his father's life? Christ, they were so screwed.

"Glenn, we can—"

"Enough bullshit." He cut her off with a wave of his gun. "I know you're the pilot."

Oh, fuck.

Her brow wrinkled in an Oscar-deserving pantomime of confused innocence. "Right. I've been flying your family for more than a year now." She raised her hand, palm out. "Are you feeling okay?"

"No, no, you beautiful, devious bitch." Glenn held his weapon inches from Caitlyn's forehead. "You're the *rescue* pilot."

CHAPTER SEVEN

DON'T REACT, CAIT. BUT GLENN'S mouth slipped into a sickly smile of triumph. She'd given away the truth.

A shiver chased down her spine.

"I wasn't one hundred percent sure," he said, "but how many white, female pilots can there be in the Caribbean?"

"So now you're going to...what?" she asked. "You think people don't know where we are tonight? Or why?"

He insolently lifted a shoulder. "Things happen in the jungle."

Her stomach turned hollow. But if he planned to kill them and make it look like an accident, he wouldn't want to shoot them now, right? Maybe they could work with that. She glanced at Kurt, who stood rigid at her side with his gaze on Glenn's backup gunman. Was he thinking the same thing?

It was her fault for getting him into this mess. She hadn't known Glenn was onto her, and she shuddered to think how he'd figured it out. Right now, though, she had to get herself and Kurt out of this alive.

This was what all that Krav Maga training she'd taken had

been for. She'd practiced disarming maneuvers for hours at a time. But even if she could execute the move effectively, what about Kurt? He was too far from the other guy to use the same tactic.

Her throat tightened. She'd have to trust him to get out of harm's way.

She counted to three. *Come on, muscle memory.*

With a deep breath, she exploded into action.

Head to the side.

Hand up to the trigger guard.

Redirect the weapon and turn.

Snap and twist the gun out of his hand.

Step back.

Holy shit, it worked! The whole action had taken a second, if that.

Glenn blinked and stared at his Glock, now in her hands. "What the fuck?"

"Don't move." Her pulse drummed in her ears as she aimed the gun at his chest, positioning herself out of reach.

Behind Glenn, his backup man was on the floor, unconscious. Kurt had figured out how to turn the tables on the guy despite the distance between them. Undoubtedly, he had skills and training far beyond hers. He hadn't just been a PJ, he'd also been part of a special tactics squadron, which was a whole other level of elite.

"What are you going to do?" Glenn taunted, his wary eyes belying his bluster. "Shoot me?"

Good question. "I'd rather not, but don't test me." The magazine was in, the trigger was forward, so at the very least there was a round in the chamber, ready to fire. And Glocks had their safety built into the trigger.

She had no desire to shoot him, but he'd be a fool to make a move.

He had the gall to smirk.

"Got any idea what to do with them now?" she asked Kurt, who was using his belt to restrain the man on the floor.

Upstairs, a floorboard squeaked, drawing Caitlyn's attention.

Glenn rushed her. Something flashed in his hand at the corner of her vision.

She pressed the trigger.

The gun kicked.

Crack.

Glenn jerked.

His jaw dropped and his blue eyes widened as he met her gaze. The knife slipped from his fingers and embedded itself into the wood floor with a *thunk*. "You…" He stared down at the scarlet stain spreading across his white shirt and sank to his knees.

Oh, God.

Caitlyn stumbled as the world around her tilted.

Was he…? Had she really just…?

Oh, God. The gun in her hands trembled.

Her pulse took off. She'd never… Not like *that*.

She tried to jettison the shock. *Get it together, Cait.* She couldn't afford to lose it now. They weren't out of danger.

But, Jesus, she'd never shot anyone point blank before. So close. So personal. His blood on her skin. Soaked into her dress.

It was self-defense. She'd had no choice. And no doubt the world would be a better place without Glenn in it, but she was no exterminator.

Her knees buckled.

"Hey." Kurt grabbed her arm and kept her on her feet, his expression full of concern. "You okay?"

"Yeah," she said, trying to clear the fog in her head and

the cotton in her ears. "I'm fine." Or she would be.

"You had no choice." He kneeled next to Glenn, who had slumped onto his side on the floor, and checked his back. "Through and through." Then, he rolled him face up and tore open Glenn's shirt to expose the oozing wound on his chest.

At the top of the stairs, a woman screamed.

Caitlyn swallowed against the rising bile in her throat and set the gun on the floor. "It's okay. I'm looking for Rose." She ran halfway up the steps on shaky legs. "And if you'd like to leave here, we can help you."

"*No.* You must go."

"But—"

"Rose is gone."

Caitlyn's stomach tumbled. Gone? "Do you know where she is? Did she get moved or…?" Caitlyn couldn't bring herself to say it.

"She disappeared last week."

The air rushed from Caitlyn's lungs. Bile rose in her throat. If Rose had run, if she was safe, wouldn't she have contacted Caitlyn or Shaylee? *No. Oh, no.*

Pulling her back to the moment, the woman shooed her away. "Guards will be coming. Go. *Now.*" She shuffled out of reach, hiding the fresh bruises on her face in the shadows. "I saw nothing," she said, and flew down the hall.

"Caitlyn," Kurt called.

On leaden feet, Caitlyn forced herself to turn away. *Gone.* "Rose isn't here." Panic beat a tattoo on her sternum. What if they were too late?

"We'll find her." Kurt sounded so sure, she almost believed him.

She needed so badly to believe him.

He had fashioned a bandage for Glenn's wound and now stood at the bottom of the stairs, holding the accomplice's weapon in his bloody hands.

"Is he—"

"Alive," Kurt said. "For now."

The man he had knocked out moaned and his eyes blinked open.

The sound of men shouting outside filtered through the dwindling rain. "Lambert's guards," she said. "We need to go. They'll shoot first, especially since—" Her gaze snagged on Glenn's bleached-out face as she raced down the stairs.

He was a vile man who had been gunning for his dad's life, but the guards would only see Lambert's son in a pool of his own blood, and her and Kurt covered in it.

Time to run.

Well, shit. So much for a rescue.

Footsteps stomped on the front porch, and bodies made shadows through the louvered glass windows in the next room.

Kurt gripped the Sig he'd commandeered and reached for Caitlyn's hand as she hit the bottom of the stairs, her face drained of color. "Let's go," he said. "Out the back."

Her gaze swept over Glenn's unconscious body and skittered away.

Kurt gave her gentle tug and she looked up. "I'm okay," she said. She clutched his hand and followed him through the utilitarian kitchen.

Outside the window, nothing moved except the moonlit shadows of windblown trees. "Stand to the side. I'm going to open the door. When I go out, stay on me and stay low."

"Copy."

Bending low at the waist, he unlocked the deadbolt and let the door swing open.

He peered around the doorjamb, weapon at the ready. No

visible threats. Behind them, the front door slammed open. No more time for a cautious retreat. "*Now.*"

He awkwardly descended the short flight of steps, Caitlyn on his heels, and raced for the cover of the thick vegetation just yards away, cool rain pelting his face.

A man appeared around the corner to their left. Kurt registered the AK in the guard's hands and fired. The man went down—probably stunned rather than injured, given that he was wearing a tactical vest—and they kept running.

Once they were hidden behind a screen of low palms and other bushes, Kurt slowed and waited for Caitlyn. Her fancy heels were more of a hindrance than his prosthetics. *Score one for technology.* Then again, she was probably less likely to catch a toe on a root or in a crevice without realizing it.

"I'd take them off," she said, gesturing to her feet, "but I think this will be even more treacherous without shoes."

He was pretty sure Dan's wife Alyssa would agree. After escaping into the jungles of St. Iz, her feet had been battered. "Any chance we can make it to your plane before they do?" Kurt asked.

"If they don't know it's us yet, maybe. If I skip the preflight check—" she wrinkled her nose "—we could be in the air within minutes."

"And if they suspect, we'll be walking into an ambush."

"Even if they don't suspect, they'll be closing all avenues of escape. And there's no cover once you enter the airfield. We'd be easy targets until we get to the plane."

"And even then…" They couldn't be in the air immediately. The propellers would take a minute to get up to speed, and they were far from quiet.

Low voices and thrashing sounds came from somewhere behind them. *Shit.* What were the chances the guards hadn't used their radios to provide Kurt and Caitlyn's description to the rest of their team already? Probably nil.

It wouldn't take long for one of them to realize who she was. Many of them had seen her around their boss for the last year.

"Does Lambert have a boat?" Kurt asked.

"Several." She waved toward the water. "But the dock is usually guarded too. We'd have to take a dinghy out to one of the bigger boats, so we couldn't exactly be stealthy. And I have no idea where the keys are."

"If we can find cover, maybe they'll pass us by. Then we can work our way around to the north side and get to the rescue car."

"Good idea. If we can't get to the van, there are bound to be limos with drivers at the ready. And you have a gun if they need convincing." She appeared to have recovered from shooting Glenn. At least for now. Being chased was a first-rate distraction.

"No need to be so bloodthirsty. I brought cash."

She grinned, and he fell a little deeper under her spell. Even rain-soaked and harried, she was breathtaking.

Remarkably, she was also calm enough to tread quietly, rather than racing in a panic through the undergrowth and giving away their position. Her green dress made for pretty good camouflage except for her arms and legs. Kurt shrugged out of his blazer and held it forward, tapping her on the shoulder. "Here, put this on. You'll be less visible."

Wordlessly, she donned the jacket and kept moving.

His gray shirt—not yet darkened by the rain—wasn't as effective, but it was better than nothing.

A few minutes later, the rain stopped, leaving only the sound of water dripping from the leaves and the roar of the ocean. Kurt slipped and slid in the mud but managed not to trip.

No matter their decision, he and Caitlyn were at a disadvantage. Lambert had enough men on his security detail to cover all the avenues of escape. But if they could take the guards by surprise, they might make it out of this alive. And if they didn't, then Kurt had never deserved the title of PJ. After all, his special tactics squadron did nothing but sensitive missions, rescuing other special forces, pilots, and high-value personnel who were stuck deep in enemy territory. It's what he had excelled at.

Of course he'd always had a team, and about six backup plans. And his own legs.

They huddled inside a nest of fern plants, cool water drizzling onto their heads from the broad leaves, and waited, breath shallow, as Lambert's men crept by in the near darkness. When several minutes passed and the men didn't return, Kurt slipped out of their hiding place and stood, listening for any signs of additional men. None of the noises were close, so he waved to Caitlyn and she joined him.

They trod carefully, as quietly as possible, keeping to the jungle, which meant they had to skirt all the way around the outside of the airfield, adding precious time to their trek. But it only took a quick glance at Caitlyn's plane to see they'd made the right choice. Several men surrounded the small aircraft, and half a dozen more were stationed around the perimeter of the fence.

They wouldn't have had a chance at escaping via air. Especially not right now, when everyone was on high alert.

When they reached the north side of the house, red and white lights flashed atop an ambulance, and several police cars had jammed themselves into the circular drive near the front entrance. The beehive of activity in the driveway served as a perfect distraction as first responders and guests milled about on the column-lined porch and spilled onto the brick walkway, voyeurs, reluctant to leave the spectacle.

And probably forced to stay by the police.

Kurt's body tingled with the awareness of Caitlyn at his side, but he pushed away the distraction and scanned the elegant cars parked along the quarter-mile private drive that led to the main gate. And more guards. They wouldn't get two feet if they tried to steal a car and drive out of here.

"I see five guards, all near the house," he said. "Do you see any I missed?" If even half of Lambert's security team was out searching for them, they were spread thin.

"No."

They needed to get off Lambert's property and find the rescue van. They didn't dare call for it to come to them, not with the police and security guards all over the place.

About a hundred yards from where he and Caitlyn waited, on the other side of the fence, two drivers leaned against their parked cars chatting. The heavy one smoked a cigarette, his foot propped on the back bumper, while the skinny one had his phone out, showing the smoking man something on his screen.

The rain started up again, just a few drops at first, quickly turning torrential. Both men swiftly sought the safety of their vehicles.

Under cover of the noisy downpour, concealed by vegetation and rain, Kurt and Caitlyn trudged toward the tall fence that lined the property. This far away, and through the rain, the people and commotion at the front of the house were blurry and dim. Most of the guests now huddled on the porch, as the paramedics brought out someone on a gurney.

"Do you think that's Glenn?" Caitlyn asked.

"Yeah. I probably gave the other guy a concussion, but I doubt he'd need a stretcher." Kurt gripped her cool, wet hand. "They're protecting him from the rain, and they didn't leave him in place for the crime scene techs, so he's probably still alive."

A short sigh that he could only interpret as relief escaped her lips.

"Let's take advantage of the commotion and the rain. To get over the fence, we need to move further down where no one will see us."

The black fence gleamed under a security light, each post shiny and slick and topped with a dangerous barb. No cross braces to serve as footholds. The climb would be difficult under any circumstances if not for one flaw. Every twenty yards or so, the fence was interrupted by a four-foot square stone column topped by a decorative cement pedestal with a planter on top.

"On my signal, run to the column and get out of sight," Kurt said. They were hidden from the house but not from the men standing watch at the front gate. "I'll give you a boost —"

"No need. I can get over that."

Of course. If anyone were going to fail at this, it would be him. Luckily, he'd spent the last six years building his upper body strength to compensate for his legs. "Okay, go."

Caitlyn sprinted to the fence, keeping to the east side of the column, out of sight. She removed her heels and his jacket and tossed them onto a bush on the other side of the fence. Then, she hiked her dress up to her hips, revealing her long, lean legs, grabbed the edge of the pedestal, and stuck one foot into a crack between stones.

Hoisting herself up, she slithered across the top of the column and jumped down on the other side. Tugging her dress down to her knees, she donned her shoes and the coat and stood watching through the rails, concealed from the row of limos and the guards by a thick hedge.

Well. He had no chance in hell of being that graceful.

Waiting until both guards were looking away, Kurt made a run for it. His shoes were too big to fit into the gaps between the stones, so he treated the top of the column like the edge of a swimming pool, pulling himself up and then pushing his torso onto the flat space next to the planter.

All that gym time had been worth something after all.

Shifting onto his butt, he lifted his legs over the fence and then rolled to slide on his stomach over the edge of the column until his shoes almost touched the ground.

He slipped in the mud and landed on his ass, but it could've been worse.

"You okay?" Caitlyn asked quietly, her tone brisk and no-nonsense.

Thank God. He didn't want her pity. "Fine." He let her help him to standing.

"That was impressive," she said, her gaze roaming over his chest and shoulders. "You're stronger."

In so many ways. And weaker in others. But who wasn't? Her attention made him want to preen. "Thanks. You were pretty amazing yourself." The image of her dress up around her hips as she scrambled over the pillar like a natural sent a bolt of heat through him. God, she was sexy.

She smiled. Even with her triumph tempered by her sadness over Rose, he had to look away and take a few breaths.

Now all they had to do was get to their van. The original plan had been for the large taxi—driven by a volunteer with The Underground—to wait for their call, pretending to be for one of the other guests that Caitlyn knew was on the list. Kurt would have entered the taxi as if leaving alone, then it would have rendezvoused with her and the others about halfway down the driveway near a stand of banana palms, leaving Kurt behind with Caitlyn to rejoin the party.

Instead, they were on their own, and even though she hid it well, he could sense her disappointment in the round of her shoulders, the fatigue around her eyes.

The fence cast a helpful shadow, and they stuck to the darkness as they hustled toward the van's waiting point. Ten minutes later, they stood on the side of the road, right where their ride should have been.

"You sure this is the place?" he asked.

"Positive."

The street was deserted in both directions. "Fabulous."

Of course the van was gone. Why had Kurt expected anything to go right? He knew better.

On the bright side, they weren't dragging along a bunch of people they were supposed to have rescued. Little consolation for Rose being God-knew-where, and the others still stuck with Lambert, clearly being mistreated.

"Back to the limos?" Caitlyn asked.

"Yeah." Kurt wiped at his wet face in vain as the rain kept coming. "I don't see what choice we have, but Lambert's guards have had more time to spread out, and the police might have joined the search. We're going to have to be extra careful."

They plodded toward the plantation, hanging in the shadows. Red lights flashed in the dark, illuminating the falling water, the trees, and the fence surrounding the large property as they approached. The road ended in a T at Lambert's street, and Kurt peered around the corner.

"Fuck. There's a roadblock."

Caitlyn snuck a glance. "Do you know how to hotwire a car?"

"Yeah, but I haven't seen any cars in this neighborhood

old enough. Anything manufactured in the last twenty years will have an alarm and a starter lock that would make it pointless."

She frowned.

He surveyed the street from behind a trailing vine growing over someone's wall. "The good news is the limos are outside the police line. The cops are set up to prevent us from leaving the plantation, which means they won't be looking for us to come back."

"They will be on alert, though," she said. "And there are probably guards along the fence line."

"Right. If we stick to the shadows, I think we can get to the limo parked on this side of the street." He looked over his shoulder at her. "You game?"

"Always."

His kind of woman. He kissed her hard and fast on the lips. Before she could utter a wide-eyed response, he crept forward. She followed until they were ten yards off the black car's bumper. Kurt hung back as Caitlyn tapped on the driver's window. The man's surprise was visible in the side mirror, but he rolled down the window.

"I'm already on a fare, ma'am. If you need a ride I can call my service for you."

Caitlyn smiled and crouched down to eye level, shielding her eyes from the rain with her hand, wearing a sweet, helpless expression Kurt had never seen on her face. "We took a wrong turn and our rental car broke down. We're due back at the port in an hour or the cruise ship will leave without us, but the rental car company can't get anyone out here fast enough," she said, her voice plaintive and distraught. She glanced at Kurt. "We can pay you cash."

Kurt nodded and hunched a little, trying to look as low-threat as possible while the man studied him in his side mirror.

"I, uh, I am not supposed to…"

"Please." Caitlyn pushed wet hair out of her eyes. "We're at the port in Ville-Nicolas, not the one in Sancoins. You might even get back before your clients realize you were gone."

The driver cast a worried look at the police barricade.

"You know what? It's okay. I'll try the other guy." She waved toward the limo in front of them.

"Three hundred."

"Oh, thank you." She managed not to look smug as she slid a stack of bills from her small purse. "How about two hundred now, two hundred when we get there?"

The driver frowned and glanced at Kurt again, but unlocked the doors with a loud click. "Okay." Maybe because they were coercing him, he didn't offer the full white-glove treatment.

Fine by Kurt. He opened the rear door and gestured for Caitlyn to slide in. Then, he joined her on the plush seats and shut out the driving rain. "Nice job," he murmured in her ear.

Caitlyn handed the money to the driver through the lowered privacy window.

"Which cruise line?" the man asked, his brown eyes skeptical in the rearview mirror, even as he started the engine.

"Caribbean Queen," Caitlyn replied without hesitation.

What would the driver do if there was no Caribbean Queen ship in the harbor?

His expression softened a bit. He maneuvered onto the road and sped away from Lambert's estate.

"What's up with all the police?" Caitlyn asked, looking over her shoulder as Kurt was, to ensure the cops didn't react.

The police officers watched, but must not have thought it odd that a hired driver might eventually leave, especially since he was outside the barricade.

The driver shrugged. "There was a shooting at the party and they're not letting anyone in or out."

She visibly shivered and Kurt scooted next to her, putting his arm around her shoulder.

"Any chance we can get the heat on back here?" he asked.

The driver fiddled with the knobs on the dash and the cool air blasting from the vents quickly turned hot.

"I thought the island was pretty safe these days," Caitlyn said with a frown. "No more rebels and a recovering economy."

"It is," the driver said, bobbing his head. "Very safe. And especially in an area like this, violence is not usual."

They sat in silence for a moment, Kurt and Caitlyn dripping water onto the vinyl seats as the warm air tried in vain to dry them out.

"Where are you coming from?" the man asked them.

Caitlyn named a restaurant that must have been in the right general area to make sense. "The seafood was worth it," she said with a satisfied smile.

"I have never eaten there, but it is a popular place."

She sat back and interlaced her fingers with Kurt's at her shoulder. He held tight, not caring if she was touching him for herself or for show.

The tap of the rain overhead, the hum of the engine, the comfortable seats, and Caitlyn pressed to his side all conspired to make him drowsy as he came down from the rush of adrenaline. But they weren't safe yet. He couldn't let his guard down.

"Thank you so much for doing this," Caitlyn said. "We spent the whole day driving around the island, and it's gorgeous, but I'd rather not get stuck here."

"Where are you from?" the man asked, his voice and

posture relaxing as they drove through the dark.

Caitlyn squeezed Kurt's hand.

"California," he said.

The driver glanced in the mirror again, his brown eyes lighting with interest. "Los Angeles?" he asked, his voice tinged with excitement. "I have always wanted to see Hollywood. And Venice Beach."

"We're from San Diego. It's about two hours south, depending on traffic. Close to Mexico."

They made small talk with the man, and reached the port in about twenty minutes.

Miraculously, the tower of a Caribbean Queen cruise ship rose above the harbor buildings, a brightly lit beacon among the smokestacks.

Caitlyn paid the driver the rest of the money and they watched him drive away before positioning themselves in a semi-private spot next to the tourist marketplace. The shops had stayed open late to take advantage of the rush of cruisers heading back to their ships for a late departure.

Removing a burner phone from her purse, she called Shaylee about the boat that was supposed to be waiting to take them and their nonexistent group to St. Lucia.

"Engine trouble," she said, zipping the burner phone into her purse. "*Shit.*"

His thought exactly. Soon every police officer on the island—and probably most of Lambert's private security team as well—would be on the hunt. And, eventually, the limo driver would realize what he'd done.

But Kurt wasn't without resources of his own. "I have an idea."

CHAPTER EIGHT

DESPITE ITS BEING ALMOST TEN p.m., the souvenir shops near the harbor were still open to accommodate last-minute shoppers who were returning from their adventures on the island. Kurt and Caitlyn quickly procured a change of clothes and left their sodden outfits in a trash bin outside the marketplace.

The rain had finally let up and it was great to be dry again. Caitlyn wore an oversized "St. Isidore *'Iz' de ting*" T-shirt and flowered board shorts with beaded flip-flops. She topped her outfit with a large rain hat to help disguise her hair, a heavy braid that dripped water down the back of her neck.

To avoid attracting attention to his prosthetics, Kurt had opted for long pants. The drawstring jammers bore colorful stripes that clashed with his surf shop T-shirt. He'd borrowed a shoehorn from one of the vendors and managed to replace his dress shoes with a pair of running shoes. Topped off with a ball cap advertising the Windward Islands cricket team, he perfectly fit the part of tacky tourist.

Transformation complete, they picked up additional clothing and sunglasses, while Kurt awaited a callback from Jason Chin, one of the guys on his team with whom Caitlyn had worked briefly three years ago. The former model might be their ticket to lying low on the island until they could figure out their next step.

They ate snow cones at a snack stand as the crowds around them hurried toward their various ships' berths.

"How did you know which cruise ships would be here?" Kurt asked, eating a scoop of the sweet ice from his cup.

"Mostly, it was an educated guess. I try to be aware of what's going on in the places I operate. It's just good business to know when the tourists are likely to be around. Now that hurricane season is almost over, visits are picking up all over the islands while the rates are still low. And St. Isidore has become increasingly popular since the new terminal opened last year."

"You spend a lot of time on St. Isidore?"

"Not really, but I've been over here several times looking for Rose. I tried all the major tourist spots and hotels. I guess now I know why I never found her."

"I'm sorry," Kurt said, laying his hand out palm up.

She curled her fingers around his, if for no other reason than to play a happy couple on holiday so they wouldn't stand out. She couldn't let herself get used to how much comfort she gained from his touch. Nor could she let herself think about how explosive their kisses had been. What should have been for show had turned into something much more serious in the space of a breath.

Just thinking about it made her hot.

Kurt's burner phone chimed, a welcome distraction. Maybe they'd get some good news.

"Hey, man. What's the word?" Kurt glanced at her with a

frown. "Are you sure he won't mind? I don't want to intrude." He listened for another minute. "Okay, thank you. I appreciate your help, Jason. Will do."

"So?" she asked.

"I have the codes for the door and the alarm. He'll give his housekeeping and maintenance staff the week off."

"Wow, generous."

They had decided that if they could make it work, staying on the island made more sense. Not only was it probably safer—and unexpected—but it would give them a chance to regroup and find a way to look for Rose and some of the other people Lambert held against their will.

It didn't hurt that they were already on Brandon Marlowe's side of the island and that his estate wasn't far from Lambert's plantation.

"Now, we just need to get there," Kurt said. "Preferably without anyone knowing where we've gone." A taxi might be convenient, but it would leave a witness to their whereabouts.

Caitlyn had been watching a young man loading boxes into a van in the alley between marketplace buildings. "If you don't mind handing over your money, I have an idea."

Kurt's forehead wrinkled but he slid his wallet across the table.

"Watch my back?" she asked, removing the bills discreetly.

His gaze flicked down her body, a look of admiration gleaming in his eyes. "Always."

Shaking her head, she slipped the wad of money into a straw tote bag she'd purchased to hold all of their new supplies and strolled into the narrow alley. Earlier, she'd noticed the kid sitting on a scooter smoking a cigarette.

"Excuse me," she said.

The boy turned from loading boxes. "Yeah?" He gave her

a wary smile.

She smiled back. "Our rental car broke down and the office is closed for the night. I know this is a weird request, but would you be willing to sell us your scooter and helmet?"

His smile dropped and his eyes widened as he glanced around as if to see if he was being punked. "You want my scooter?" His dark brows lowered in confusion as he gestured to the bright blue vehicle gleaming under the overhead lights.

"Yes." She lowered her voice. "I have cash. U.S."

His expression changed to one of guarded interest. "How much?" He eyed her bag and she tightened her grip.

"How much do you want?"

He bit his lower lip and called to his boss, waving the older man over. They exchanged words in the local creole, which had more of a French influence than Bajan, so she only understood a few words.

The kid turned back to Caitlyn. "One thousand."

Jesus. Kurt had come prepared, but she didn't know if she should use up the majority of his cash on this. Then again, without inconspicuous transportation, they had nothing.

"I can give you eight hundred," she said.

The boy looked at the shiny bike for a minute. "Okay."

Thank God. Hopefully the scooter ran as well as it looked.

He unlocked the seat and lifted it to reveal a storage space with an additional helmet. He removed a couple of personal items, stuffing them into the pockets of his cargo shorts, and then handed her the keys.

The older man, his curly dark hair infused with gray, watched carefully as she withdrew money from her bag shielding it from view of any onlookers.

She counted out the money and discreetly handed it over.

"You've cleaned us out," she said. These guys seemed nice and honest, but there was no need to advertise that she still had hundreds of dollars left. "Thank you so much. I really appreciate it."

"Bring it back when you're done, maybe I'll buy it back from you for a discount." He grinned.

She chuckled. "I'll think about it."

She waved at Kurt, and he joined her as the men went back to loading the van with trinkets and souvenirs from their stall.

"Nicely done," Kurt said. "Let's hope this thing runs."

"And has gas," she said, stuffing her bag into the storage space under the padded seat. "Nothing's open right now."

Since she had a better idea where they were going, and was used to driving on the left, Caitlyn took the front and Kurt settled behind her, one muscled arm looped around her waist. Despite his loose hold, the contact made it hard to breathe.

Within minutes they were speeding—well, not exactly speeding, since the little bike couldn't top fifty-five kilometers per hour—away from the port toward Brandon Marlowe's oceanfront home.

As the crow flies, he only lived about three miles from Lambert, and it was unnerving to head back toward that evil man's home. But if they did find a way to raid his place, being so close would give them an advantage.

Plus, she doubted Lambert or the local law enforcement would expect her and Kurt to stick around the island, let alone be within a five-mile radius of the scene of the crime.

Her mind faltered at the memory of Glenn lying on the floor, his blood draining from his body and splattered across her green dress. The rain had washed her and her clothes clean, but she could almost feel the blood on her skin, as if it would permanently stain. Was it because she had known him personally? No matter how much she had disliked him, and no matter how despicable he was, she couldn't seem to get over the fact that she was responsible for that kind of damage.

Yes, he'd lunged at her with a knife. Every cop, and anyone who'd studied hand-to-hand combat, knew a knife could be just as deadly as a handgun, maybe more so. Rationally, she knew she had done what she had to do, but it was little comfort.

How did men like Scott Kramer—one of Steele's snipers —look through the scope of his rifle, stare his target right in the face, and press the trigger? Then again, how did any of these guys kill when necessary?

She wasn't innocent. She knew that. And yet, still, she was struck with the difference between shooting at a nameless, faceless attacker, and the up-close and personal fight with Glenn. It should matter to her just as much that she may have taken lives from afar, but as much she didn't want it to, being face-to-face made a difference.

With a sigh, she jettisoned her unproductive thoughts. She'd made a wrong turn and hit a dead end, and she couldn't use their phones for GPS. Before getting on the scooter, they'd both tossed their phones to avoid tracking and surveillance. Once they'd used the burners to call known associates—Kurt to secure Brandon's house for their use and provide Tara with an update, and Caitlyn to give Shaylee the bad news about Rose and ask her neighbor, Jade, to take care of Rockley—the devices had become a liability.

So, now she had to wing it.

Having landed on Marlowe's runway in the past helped with the general location, but she didn't know the exact turn-by-turn directions on the ground.

Backtracking, she made a few more wrong turns before finally pulling into the driveway on the north side of the actor's house. His home sat at the end of a quiet street, less than a hundred yards from the beach.

Waves made shushing sounds against the shore, and bugs and frogs croaked into the night. The two-story home was modest by Hollywood standards, but fairly large for St. Isidore, probably about three thousand square feet on two levels. The exterior was lit like the Lincoln Memorial, showing off its white stucco walls and dark green shutters, all the windows lined up in a classic colonial style.

It was quite different from Lambert's villa with its wide porches, Corinthian columns, and archways. Then again, how much space did one man really need? Probably, Marlowe had been more drawn in by the location and surrounding lands that gave him privacy than by the house itself.

She looked around, but didn't see any paparazzi lurking in the bushes.

"All the stories I've heard about this place," Kurt said, "I finally get to see for myself."

She parked on the outer edge of the driveway close to the house, removed her tote bag and stowed their helmets, and pushed the scooter under an overhanging palm to conceal it somewhat until they could get into the garage. "You get to enter the lair of Aible Ranctos himself," she said in a mock awe-tinged voice.

"Are you a big fan?" Kurt asked, his expression giving away nothing.

Three years ago, she hadn't even heard of Brandon Marlowe. After he helped out Steele, she'd decided to change that. "I liked the whole *Sinzian Empire* series, but the books were better." The *Sinzian Empire* movies were the hottest thing since *Star Wars* or *Lord of the Rings*, and the epic's primary actors had become instant superstars, growing up over the twelve-year span during which the films were released.

Marlowe, who played Aible Ranctos, was a fan favorite for his good looks and athletic physique, but he somehow managed to stay off the tabloid's front pages. Maybe because the series' two other stars had gone a little wild and now attracted most of the media attention.

Kurt turned for the door, his gaze scanning the dark street. "I haven't read the books, but I liked the movies," he said grudgingly.

She stifled a smile and followed him up the sidewalk, her neck tingling. Despite the private location, anyone could be lurking in the bushes, watching as she stood fully exposed under the porch light in front of the carved wooden double door as Kurt punched in the code.

The lock opened with a mechanical whir and they were in.

After scoping out the house for threats and egress options, and stowing their purchases upstairs, Kurt sat next to Caitlyn on a stool at the breakfast bar in Brandon Marlowe's kitchen, sipping water from a glass. His legs were grateful for the break after the evening's exertions. "This is kind of surreal."

"I know. It's actually weirder for me this time around, now that I know who this guy is. Last time we had a crowd of people and I wasn't sticking around. Now I feel like I'm trespassing."

"Yeah." He didn't know why the actor was so willing to help them out, but he needed to have Tara send the guy a gift when this was over. "At least he uses timers, so it won't look weird to any neighbors if the lights are on in the evening."

"True." She set her palms flat on the granite counter.

"Now what?"

"Tara's going to contact Valerie first thing tomorrow, and they'll both start digging into anything to do with Lambert that can help us."

"Valerie works for you now?"

"Yeah. She's our resident computer guru-slash-hacker. I don't know how we ever worked without her."

Caitlyn rested her elbows on the counter and rubbed her hands down her face. "I hate this. I feel helpless and useless, and every other 'less' you can think of."

He itched to comfort her, but he kept his hands to himself. If he touched her again, he wouldn't want to stop. "Tomorrow, I'll pick up a computer or tablet and some burner phones so you can start feeling useful. I have the Wi-Fi password, but there's no computer here."

Rolling her head to look at him, she asked, "Why just you?"

"Because the police are looking for a couple. And you're far too recognizable."

"And you're not?"

"I'm a white guy with brown hair. In the tourist areas, I'll blend right in."

She raised a skeptical eyebrow. "Only if you cover up all those muscles."

He warmed a little. But she was right. If his bulk looked like fat he'd be less noticeable and less intimidating. "Point taken."

"A lot of stores on the island are closed on Sundays. Your best bet will be to find something near the cruise ships."

"Good to know. I hadn't even thought of that. We're spoiled back home, and not necessarily in a good way."

"Yeah. It took me a while to get used to, but now it's one of the things I love about Barbados. I can get anything I need on the island or online, but the lifestyle is simpler. Less cluttered with stuff, not so crowded."

Kurt sipped his water. "I like DC, and I'm used to the conveniences, but it's hectic. I have to escape every few weeks."

Caitlyn twirled her water glass on the counter. "I don't know if I can sleep, but I'm about ready to slide right off this stool."

He chuckled. "Ditto." Rising, he double-checked that the alarm system was on and they went upstairs.

The house had three enormous bedrooms, all on the second floor. The long front half of the house was taken up by the master bedroom and bathroom, while the back of the house was split into two, with a guest bath and the stairs between them.

There were enough beds and pullout couches to sleep an entire squadron.

"Why don't you take the this one?" Caitlyn asked, standing in the doorway to a yellow room with two king beds. "More space for you to spread out."

"Actually, the queen beds in the other room are lower to the ground. They'll be easier for me to get in and out of." Once he took off his legs.

"Oh. Right. No problem."

They said goodnight and he went to the green bedroom while she headed for the bathroom. He dug the chargers and batteries for his legs out of his pocket and placed them on the dresser. He didn't go anywhere without them, because running out of juice for his legs could ruin a man's day. The batteries could last up to five days, but nightly charging was recommended. He chose not to test it.

Luke thought it was cool that he could plug in his legs to recharge, like a robot or something. He loved his nephew's perspective on the world.

The latch on the bathroom door unlocked with a *click* and the door to Caitlyn's room opened and closed again. He set the Sig he'd stolen on the nightstand and entered the bathroom, locking the door to her side. He found a stash of new toothbrushes and various toiletries—Marlowe was ready for surprise guests—and happily brushed his teeth and washed his face.

Finally, he sat on the toilet to remove his legs. At least he had privacy, though he'd still prefer to be sharing a bed with Caitlyn.

Hung up, much? Stupid, stupid, stupid. This was hardly the time to make a move.

He broke the vacuum seal on his sockets before he slid them off his stumps and set the legs aside. Then, he massaged each limb the way Caitlyn was probably rubbing her feet after running around in heels all night. Sweet relief.

With a damp washcloth, he did a full-body wipe down, and then moved his prostheses into the bedroom so they wouldn't startle Caitlyn if she used the bathroom later.

At midnight, he was still staring at the ceiling, listening to the wind and waves, restless sounds that matched his mood. Despite the cool air whispering through the vents, a light layer of sweat covered his skin, and he'd pushed all the sheets to the bottom of the bed.

Every few minutes, a faint rustle came from Caitlyn's room and the bedsprings squeaked. Was she a turbulent sleeper or was she struggling too?

Two hours later, a crash woke Kurt from a hazy half-sleep. He sat bolt upright, his pulse slamming, and reached for his weapon. Had he been dreaming?

On the other side of the wall, the wooden floor creaked.

Kurt slid from the bed and cut through the bathroom—

far quicker than going around and down the hall. Flinging open the door to her room, he raised his weapon and did a visual sweep.

The outside security lights cast enough of a glow through the shutters that he could see Caitlyn standing next to the bed in a long T-shirt, gaping at him. No one else was in sight.

"Sorry," he said, lowering the weapon. "I…heard a noise." …*am an idiot.*

"It's okay." She grimaced. "I bumped the alarm clock and it fell off the nightstand." Sitting on the edge of the mattress, she said, "Did I wake you?"

He shook his head. "I don't know. As exhausted as I am, I'm having trouble sleeping."

"Me too." She shifted to sit against the headboard and hugged her knees to her chest, wrapping the shirt over her legs. "I can't stop thinking about Rose, wondering where she is, if she's okay." Her chin dropped to her knees. "If only I'd acted sooner. I should have hired your guys to get her back and damn the consequences."

She couldn't have known Rose would be gone, but he'd be suffering the same guilt in her shoes. No point in arguing.

He wore only boxers, stumps bared, but she hadn't asked him to leave, so he slipped onto the sofa and set the gun to his side.

Caitlyn looked her fill, her gaze lingering on the tattoo on his chest, but said nothing.

"Tell me something about Rose," he said.

Her head lifted. "What do you mean?"

He shrugged. "I know she's a graphic artist, you have different dads, she has a girlfriend… I don't know. Tell me a story. Or whatever you can think of." She wasn't going to stop thinking about Rose, but he could help her quit dwelling on the unknown.

Caitlyn stared at her toes in thought for several minutes. "When I was fourteen and Rose was eleven, my mom's brother Gary came to visit from San Francisco right before school started." Her voice was low and intimate and made Kurt wish he was closer. "He had rented a shiny red convertible that he worried about parking in our neighborhood, the nicest car we'd ever been in. My mom had to work, but Gary took me and Rose and Mike out to lunch and bought us toys and candy and books. He fed us ice cream and French fries from room service and let us watch HBO in his posh hotel room.

"It had been so long since a man gave us any attention, showed us any love. Even when Rose and Mike's dad was around, he treated us more like goldfish than children, making sure our basic needs were met, but otherwise ignoring us. I thought Gary was amazing. He could eat whatever he wanted, drive wherever he wanted. He could afford to fly from California to see us. I'd never even been out of Colorado Springs.

"On the third day, he bought us swimsuits and took us to play in the hotel pool. I had taken swim lessons as a kid, but Rose and Mike had never been in water deeper than a bathtub, so they stayed in the shallow end splashing around."

Caitlyn's jaw hardened and she looked toward the window as if she could see through the closed shutters. "I loved being underwater. Until I started flying, that insulated, muffled, weightless world became my favorite escape."

He knew exactly what she meant. Swimming had kept him sane over the years.

Blowing out a harsh breath, she said, "I was supposed to be helping watch my sister and brother, but I was doing handstands and swimming along the bottom of the pool like a shark, oblivious, having the time of my life. When I came up for air, Rose was nowhere in sight. She and Mike had been cannonballing into the pool but she jumped in too close to the deep end and the water was over her head. She panicked and flailed, even though she probably could have walked to shallower water."

"I remember that awful feeling from combat driver training," Kurt said. "It's bad enough when you're prepared for it. I can't imagine going through it as a kid. What happened?"

"Gary was reading a book on a lounge chair, but when Mike started screaming he jumped in and dragged Rose to the shallow end. Thank God she wasn't under long enough to pass out or anything, just to swallow some water and freak out, but it changed everything." She fell silent, seemingly lost in her thoughts.

"How so?"

"Well, the fire department and police responded, they called Child Protective Services, who took us away for a week, placing each of us in different foster homes. The investigators finally gave us back, but Rose and Mike were traumatized, and I knew I could have prevented all of it if I'd just paid attention like Gary asked me to."

Kurt shook his head, but she pressed on.

"I found out years later that he was a registered sex offender and CPS had gotten involved because my mom knew about it and left us with him anyway. But it sounds worse than it was. He'd been caught having sex with his seventeen-year-old girlfriend when he was eighteen. They were both seniors in high school, but her father flipped out and pressed for statutory rape."

"That's harsh. Seems like a stupid way to potentially ruin someone's life."

"Yeah." She bit her lip and stared at her toes. "I think we

were all ruined in our own ways. Rose never went in the water again. She wouldn't even come to my swim meets. Hell, she lives on an island now, but still won't get within twenty yards of the ocean." She grimaced. "My reaction was just as bad." She briefly closed her eyes and let out a long breath. "I backed away completely. Up until that point, Rose and I had been pretty close, but the whole experience scared me half to death. I felt guilty for letting her almost drown and for bringing CPS down on our family's head. She was a constant reminder of my failure. And initially, I think she blamed me too."

"It wasn't your fault," Kurt said. "You were just a kid."

Caitlyn toyed with the edge of her shirt and shrugged off his words. "I also realized how much I cared about her, how much it would hurt if something happened to her—the same way it hurt when our dads left—and I... I tried to stop caring." A tear slipped down Caitlyn's cheek, the dim light sparkling in its wake. "I started high school two weeks later, and I used every excuse I could find not to spend time with her. Homework, new friends, sports, clubs. Why would a freshman want to hang out with a sixth-grader anyway, right? She pulled back too, stopped seeking me out to talk or play. By the time I left for basic, we hardly knew each other."

"I'm sorry," Kurt said. Rose wasn't the only one she'd kept arm's length. Even as much as Caitlyn had let down her guard with him and Terrell, she'd held part of herself back.

"When she came to Barbados," Caitlyn said, "things were better. We both made more of an effort, but she was as skittish as I was. Probably because she could sense I wasn't willing to go all in." Caitlyn pressed her palms to her eyes. "What if I've lost her, Kurt? How will I ever forgive myself?"

There were no words, so he held out his hand.

CHAPTER NINE

CAITLYN WOKE SLOWLY, THE GOLDEN light of sunrise peeking through the slats of the shutters, and immediately wished she could fall back into ignorant oblivion. Good God. She had *cried* last night. And worse yet, in front of Kurt.

What the hell was wrong with her? She rarely shed tears, and sure as hell not in public. He seemed to bring out all of her vulnerabilities.

Like now, for example. Not only had she dragged the bedspread over to the couch and let him comfort her, she had fallen asleep in his arms. Then, at some point during the night, he had moved onto his back and now she lay sprawled across his muscled torso, using his broad chest as a pillow. He was warm and solid and delicious. Her legs were twined with his thighs and his erection pressed against her hip, thick and hard.

How easy it would be to move over a few inches, push aside her panties, and make them both happy. Her stomach dipped. If their earlier kisses were any indication, he wouldn't protest. But it wouldn't be fair to lead him on. He wanted a wife and a family, and she could offer neither.

The tears burned again. Goddammit.

Trying to avoid jostling him, she let her right leg slide down until her foot hit the floor. Then she pushed against the back of the couch to lift herself up, the bedspread pooling at her feet.

His dark eyes opened and he stared up at her, blinking once or twice before he jolted upright and crossed his wrists over his lap. "Morning," he said, his voice rusty.

"Sorry." She tugged on the hem of her T-shirt and folded her arms, though it was probably too late to hide the see-through nature of the thin cotton. "I didn't mean to wake you."

He glanced at his watch, his cheeks turning pink. "No problem. I'm usually up by now."

Her gaze strayed to his residual limbs—the correct term for his stumps, according to the research she'd done after he told her about his injuries. Last night, it had been too dark to see them clearly, and she had expected much worse. Basically, his thighs looked…normal, muscular, in fact, until tapering just above where his knees would be. The skin at the end was hairless and stretched, and each leg had been rounded off into a pillowy shape with a shiny scar along the bottom.

"It's weird, isn't it?"

"I'm sorry." She was stuck in apology mode now. "I didn't mean to stare."

He shook his head. "It's okay. I'd rather you stare than be afraid to look."

She swallowed. "Does it hurt to walk on them?"

"Not anymore."

He didn't want or need pity, but she still hated that he'd gone through so much pain and struggle. "How long were you in the hospital?"

"In-patient and out-patient combined, I lived at Walter Reed for almost two years."

Jesus. "That long?" She couldn't even imagine.

"I don't know how I would've gotten through it if Sara hadn't quit her job and moved in with me."

Because their parents had died, and he'd had no one else to advocate for him. Sara was a much better sister than Caitlyn had ever been. "That's where she met your physical therapist?"

"Yeah, Soham. He makes her happy, so I let him live." Kurt gave her a cheeky smile.

Her chest constricted. "I'm glad *you* lived." As if she would have wished otherwise. The words sounded stupid as soon as they came out of her mouth.

"Me too." His smile turned into a full-blown sexy grin. "Otherwise, I wouldn't be sitting here half naked after spending the night with you."

Half naked and sexy as hell. Up close she could clearly see that the tattoo on his left pec was a curling ribbon emblazoned with "That Others May Live." The second half of the pararescue motto was a summary of Kurt in four words, and it only made him more desirable.

Her cheeks burned. Damned fair skin. "All these comfortable beds and we ended up on the couch. I hope it wasn't too bad for you," she said, keeping her voice light.

He laughed, deep and playful. "I will happily sleep under you anywhere, anytime, Braveheart," he said, invoking the stupid play on her last name Terrell had been so proud of.

"Oh, God." She rolled her eyes and bent to grab the bedspread and wrap it around her shoulders. With luck, the move hid the jolt of lust that shot straight to her core at his suggestion. "*Men.*" Tamping down her unwanted attraction, she straightened. "Do you need to use the toilet?"

"Go for it. I can wait. If I get desperate there are two other restrooms in the house."

Snatching up a change of clothes, she threw the quilt on the bed and shut herself into the bathroom without a backward glance.

Fifteen minutes later, feeling somewhat refreshed, she scrounged through Brandon's cupboards and started a pot of oatmeal and, more importantly, a pot of coffee.

Kurt joined her soon after, back to full height. Had he waited for her to leave the room this morning so he wouldn't have to walk on his residual limbs in front of her? He'd done it last night, but it had been dark then, and he'd thought she was in danger.

As much as she rejected the idea of being a damsel in distress who needed a man, the memory of him rushing into her room ready to fight for her sent a ripple of pleasure through her chest.

"I'll pick up some groceries later if I can find anything open," he said, breaking into her reverie.

"Good idea. I hate raiding this guy's cupboards, and there's not much here anyway."

While the oats simmered, Kurt switched on the enormous flat-screen TV that hung on the wall across from the sectional sofa. A local morning news show talked about another tropical storm developing to the southeast. This year, the Atlantic had already seen more than its fair share of hurricanes, with multiple storms devastating Puerto Rico and the Leeward Islands, along with Mexico, Texas, and Florida.

Barbados and St. Isidore had been spared this time around, but everyone was on edge about it. St. Iz was only now starting to recover from a hurricane followed by a series of earthquakes three years ago.

When the coffee finished, Caitlyn poured herself a cup

and added a smidge of powdered creamer and sugar. "How do you like your caffeine?" she asked Kurt.

"Strong and hot, one sugar, no cream."

She prepared his cup and brought it to him where he stood in front of the television looking sinfully handsome with damp hair and dark stubble. He even smelled good.

"Thanks." He lifted the mug in a little salute. "Unfortunately, I may not be able to get any of my guys here for a few days. There's a tropical storm sitting off the mid-Atlantic, and airports up and down the coast are shut down due to high winds."

"You were planning to bring your team here? For what?" They hadn't even talked about it.

He glanced at her, eyebrows darting up as he took a sip of coffee. "To increase security around this house. And so they could be ready to help when we figure out where Rose is."

Caitlyn sighed. She had fought so hard for control over her life that it was hard to step back and let him take charge, even though they needed all the help they could get. But she didn't need to antagonize him. He was, as always, trying to help.

"I'd appreciate it if you could keep me in the loop."

"No problem. I didn't mean to cut you out, I'm just used to—"

"Being in charge."

His self-deprecating smile softened her more than she liked. "Yeah. I've gotten used to being the boss."

She scoffed. "No, you've gotten used to being the savior."

He didn't even balk at her characterization, he just smiled. "PJ training only made me more insufferable. But then I lost my legs." He huffed out a laugh. "That'll teach you who's really in charge."

Any remaining irritation leached out of her. Based on his faraway expression, he hadn't said it to garner sympathy or pity or even to sway her. He was merely musing.

"I was at the mercy of the hospital staff and my injuries for so long... I hoarded every piece of my world that I could control. How hard I worked in physical therapy, how much I practiced with my prosthetics, what I ate, what I read, what I watched, my attitude. Starting Steele Security let me take charge again. Not just of my team, but of my life."

And couldn't she understand that? Caitlyn cringed inwardly. Kurt's injuries had made him more vulnerable than she could imagine, especially looking at him now, standing tall and strong. He had to hate it. He'd always been the protector, the one who swooped in to save others when they were weak and helpless. There was nothing in the world worse than being knocked down, defenseless against the vultures, ripe for others to take advantage.

Which was why she so carefully guarded her own independence. "And it proves just how uncreative you are at naming things," she said with a straight face.

He laughed and seemed to snap back to the present. "You mean like Brevard Charters?"

She smiled against her will. He had her there. "Touché."

Their gazes met and she melted. How bad would it be to kiss him for no good reason? Just being near him made her breathless. She couldn't run from it, but maybe she could make him feel just as helpless and vulnerable and out of control.

She took a step back, forced herself to lean away, and broke eye contact. The fake engagement was irrelevant. They no longer had a reason to play the happy couple. And yet...

She didn't want to desire him. She didn't want to need anyone. But her body and her heart—no, not her heart, never that—hadn't gotten the message.

Kurt frowned and something flickered in his dark eyes. Disappointment?

Caitlyn cleared her throat, "I don't know if you have some grand plan, and I know you're better at this than I am, but I want and need to be included in the process. Otherwise I'll go crazy."

He nodded. "I understand. We'll come up with a plan together."

"Thank you." She managed not to kiss him.

First step, find Rose. Simple.

Kurt studied the news, not hearing a word, far too aware of the woman next to him. The couch hadn't been all that comfortable last night, but with Caitlyn draped across his body, he hadn't cared. He'd lain awake for hours, unable to sleep, intoxicated and tortured by the feel of her soft skin, her breasts pressed to his chest, and her sweet scent.

The sensation had settled on him, an invisible layer of dust that wouldn't wash away, and now anytime she moved near, his heart sped up, his throat turned dry.

She'd seen his stumps this morning, and she hadn't been disgusted by them. Still, he'd waited until she went to the restroom to slide down from the couch and walk to his room.

His sister, Soham, and the nurses at the hospital had all assured him that the loss of height didn't diminish him, that anyone who truly cared about him wouldn't care about his legs. But it wasn't so much being short that bothered him as the constant reminder of his vulnerability. No matter how strong he got in the gym, or how smart he was in any area of his life, he had lost the sense of invincibility that one has to cultivate as a PJ.

Neither he nor his teammates ever believed themselves

bulletproof, but he wouldn't have been able to leap from a plane or ride a helo into a village taking enemy fire if he'd been thinking about his mortality every moment. Now he was faced with it every day, every morning when he pulled back the covers and every night when he removed his legs.

But he had lived. And after the initial shock and pain and anger that had come with his injuries, he was grateful for that. If nothing else, he had learned the fragility of life and how little he could count on tomorrow. He'd learned how important it was to go after what you wanted because life gave no promises.

Which was why he was willing to risk emotional evisceration for a second chance with Caitlyn. She was worth it.

For a brief moment when she'd joked with him about his company name, Kurt had thought she was going to lean in and kiss him the way his body was begging to be kissed. His muscles had gone rigid with the anticipation of tasting her lips again, every nerve on alert. But then something in her expression had changed and the thread had snapped, and she was all business, trying to wrest a shred of control from this crazy situation.

He sighed. His need to be in charge had blinded him to the fact that he hadn't consulted her. This was her show. He might have the resources to help, but she had put everything in motion, and she deserved to have input and full say on everything they did and everyone they involved. As long as he didn't feel her decisions put him or anyone else in unnecessary danger, he would support her one hundred percent.

It was tougher than it should be to take a backseat, but— as his sister kept telling him—he could learn a little humility. Sara knew his heart was in the right place, but maybe Caitlyn assumed he was an arrogant asshole. Sometimes he didn't even know why she and Terrell had put up with him when they were in the maintenance squadron together.

Maybe she knew she could trust him with her life. Maybe she instinctively got that part of him.

But did she realize much of a fool he was? Specifically, how much of a fool he was, and always had been, for *her*?

She had returned to the kitchen, and was now dishing oatmeal into bowls. He turned off the TV. Outside, the ocean caressed the shore with an insistent shushing sound, and the palm trees that divided the backyard from the airfield rustled in the wind. Inside, the house was quiet as they sat together at the breakfast bar and slowly ate the hot cereal, which she'd flavored with raisins and cinnamon and walnuts.

"Thanks for cooking."

"Don't get used to it."

His laugh faded quickly. He wanted to get used to everything about her.

The doorbell rang. Kurt jerked at the sound. Who the hell would come knocking at seven a.m.?

He pushed to standing and slipped softly into the front hall where a video monitor showed two St. Isidore police officers standing on the front porch. *Shit.*

Caitlyn had followed to investigate and at his signal, she tiptoed close to him, staying out of the line of sight of windows, and careful not to cast a shadow across the peephole in the door. The shutters were mostly closed, but they weren't a solid screen.

Afraid to move lest they make any noise to give away their presence, they huddled in the hall, watching the monitor. Caitlyn's green eyes were wide with concern but she didn't tremble, or bite her lip. She stood strong and ready to take action. A warrior goddess with the beauty to match.

Had someone tipped off the police, or were they going door to door? Or was it unrelated to him and Caitlyn altogether?

Logically, if the police knew they were there, they'd have brought a bigger team. And they wouldn't have come politely to the front door. Then again, maybe the house was surrounded by SWAT.

A loud knock echoed in the hall. She flinched at the noise, but didn't make a sound.

His heart pounded as time slowly ticked forward, an eternity in the space of a minute.

Voices rumbled through the door, their words muffled, and then finally retreated as the men on camera left the porch. Silence descended on the house.

Another minute passed, interrupted only by the sound of Kurt's pulse in his ears.

He crashed as the adrenaline drained from his veins and he gripped the wall. He met Caitlyn's gaze and saw the same jittery relief wash over her.

"Too close," she whispered.

"Not close enough," he said. Then he tugged her against him and kissed her.

Caitlyn froze in shock at the unexpected lip lock and then sank into the kiss, sank into Kurt's warm, strong embrace, and let herself fall into the delicious whirlwind. They came together with a spark, igniting like flash paper. She'd never experienced anything even close to this with another man.

Lips, teeth, tongue, hands, all hungry and searching, seeking and driving them closer. Their bodies fused together.

His breath was her breath, his heartbeat hers.

She pressed him to the wall slipping her leg between his thighs while wrapping the other one around his hips, bringing them together where it mattered most.

He groaned deep in his chest and flipped them around so that she was caged between him and the cool plaster. Her hands slid beneath his shirt, eager for the feel of his hot skin against her fingertips. He was so goddamned sexy with all his hard muscles and quiet strength. She couldn't even remember why she didn't want this. He kissed her face, her neck, nipped at her shoulder, pushed aside the collar of her shirt and worked his way down her chest. She willed her clothes to disintegrate, or maybe combust, leaving her instantly naked and ready.

Ding dong.

Shit. *What now?*

Kurt froze, his muscles rigid, his breath coming hard and as fast as hers. They both looked at the monitor on which a mail courier was visible, placing a package against the door with a thump before retreating.

"Jesus." Pushing away from the wall, Kurt disentangled himself from her grasp and ran a hand through his hair, staring at her with dark eyes full of desire and... regret? "That was—"

"Maybe what we both needed," she finished.

His eyebrows rose.

She lifted one shoulder. "You know, adrenaline can have that effect." She was such a liar. Maybe even a coward.

His face blanked. "Adrenaline. Right." He took a deep breath, turning away from her to peer through the viewer in the door.

Caitlyn stared at his broad back, still able to feel his warm skin and the contours of his muscles under her fingertips. Her entire body was keyed up from their red-hot make-out session. What had she been thinking kissing him back? Why hadn't she pushed him away?

Maybe because he was the best kisser ever. Or maybe it was because kissing him was almost better than flying. She didn't go home with a guy every month or anything, but she hadn't been celibate. She had kissed other men, she'd had sex with other men, but none of them affected her like Kurt.

It made him far too dangerous. She couldn't risk getting emotionally tangled up with him, giving him that kind of power over her. Which meant rejecting him again, and it fucking sucked. Kurt was not for her. Not for the short term and definitely not for the long term. The loss of "what could be" was nothing compared the pain of loving someone and losing them. Case in point, her sister. Lambert hadn't intentionally taken Rose to hurt her, but the end result was the same.

If she fell in love with Kurt and he left—because that's what men did—or died, she'd never recover.

She nearly snorted at her assumption that she would live long enough for it to matter. Lambert presented himself publicly as a jovial man, but she had gravely injured his only son. That would be unforgivable for anyone, and he could be ruthless.

Kurt turned away from the door, and for second she could swear there was a residual heat in his eyes.

An answering fire flared deep in her belly, and she looked away to break the connection. "Maybe this isn't the best place to hide out after all."

"This is why I wanted some of my guys here. They can keep watch, warn us when someone's coming, help us fight off any threats."

"But they can't get here anytime soon. Not with all the airports shut down."

"No." He followed her back to the kitchen. "Once we have phones and a computer, I can get Valerie to look into

Lambert. If there's anything online that can help us, she'll find it. Tara will work on getting a few guys out here, and whatever else we need."

"You're lucky to have such a loyal team."

"I am," he said. "I have good friends."

Rockley was the most loyal friend Caitlyn had. How pathetic. But it was her own fault. She couldn't avoid connections and still expect to have a stable full of people ready to sacrifice for her.

Except Kurt was here doing just that, despite how she'd treated him when they were stationed in Oklahoma. He deserved so much better. If she could take back how much she'd hurt him…

"I didn't cheat on you when you were at Indoc," she blurted.

CHAPTER TEN

CAITLYN'S WORDS WERE SO OUT of context that it took Kurt a second to comprehend them. And then all the long-held anger and the leaden sense of betrayal collapsed over him with the force of a tsunami. Twelve years evaporated in an instant.

"Immaculate conception, was it?" he snapped. They may have only shared a few kisses the night before he left for training, but he'd ridden high on the memory during the ten weeks he was gone, parlaying it into much, much more.

Only to return to find out she was six weeks pregnant. Simple math.

Her face turned bright red.

Shit. He sighed. Hadn't he moved past this? "I know we didn't have an explicit understanding or anything, but I—"

"Aaron raped me."

Kurt's chin jerked back and he gaped like a fish stuck on dry sand, suddenly unable to breathe. "He…" Christ. Kurt's blood heated as rage pounded through his veins, useless and inadequate. "That fucker." He forced his hands to unclench.

His violent mood wouldn't do either of them any good now. "God, Caitlyn, I'm so sorry." Could he be more impotent? "Why didn't you tell me? Why didn't you *report* him?"

She hugged her middle. "And relive that horrible moment over and over only to have it all shoved under the rug? No, thank you. I just wanted to move on. And I have."

"I'm sorry," he sighed and raked his hair. "I didn't mean to attack you." More than anything, she hated to be vulnerable. He knew that. But still… Jesus. If he'd known, he never would have walked away from her after such a trauma. He'd been nursing his broken heart, feeling like the injured party, totally unaware that she'd been violated in the worst way. Never mind that she hadn't told him, shouldn't he have sensed something was wrong?

Instead he'd taken her at face value, letting her drive him right out of her life.

If he could go back, he'd hunt Aaron down and break his fucking neck.

"Besides," she said. "I let him in to my room. We had a history. He was a freaking *cop*. It was my word against his, and you know the military doesn't have a great track record with that kind of thing. You really think anyone in charge would have believed me?"

Sadly, no. Assholes like Aaron usually got away with it, and even if they were caught with irrefutable evidence, they often skated with minimum sentences. Especially if there was even a hint the woman had "asked for it." Given the shaming and skepticism victims often faced, he understood her reluctance to seek justice.

"You could have told me," Kurt said softly. "I would've kept your secret. I would have been there for you. No expectations."

Her gaze didn't waver. "I know."

And still she'd chosen not to. He could've easily taken that personally, but that would be selfish. Especially given that he would have left her again even if she'd been willing to pursue a relationship—friendship or otherwise—after what she'd been through. PJ training lasted at least eighteen months and he'd just been getting started. Near-constant deployment would have followed. He'd have rarely been home. She had owed him nothing.

Except, just now, she'd given him something anyway. Her trust. And after a dozen years of believing otherwise, he knew she hadn't tossed him aside the minute he left for Indoc. She hadn't lied to him in the way he'd thought.

"Why are you telling me now?" he asked.

She licked her lips and sighed. "Because despite what you thought I did, you're here. I hurt you, and I'm sorry. That's the last thing I wanted to do, but at the time I was too wrapped up in my own pain to care. I certainly wasn't in a place to pick up where we left off. Letting you believe the worst of me was easier than telling you the truth." She lifted one shoulder with studied indifference. "And I was afraid of what you might do."

Her concern over his reaction was justified. He would've hunted the motherfucker down and probably ended up in jail. He wouldn't even have regretted giving up the Air Force and the PJs if it meant Caitlyn got justice.

"Did you talk to *anyone*?" he asked.

"No. You're the first."

His heart folded in on itself. She had suffered all this alone. "Thank you for trusting me now."

She nodded and stared at the wall behind him, arms crossed.

"I wish to God you *had* cheated on me," he said. "I wish it had been that simple and harmless." Between her dad, stepdad, and Aaron, it was no wonder she didn't trust men to treat her right. "I would gladly take that hurt a million times over if I could take back what happened to you."

"Yeah." Her emerald gaze met his. "Well."

Right. He couldn't. He was being stupid. Wanting to fix and save her when it was far too late to do either. And not his place, for that matter.

What she needed was for him not to show pity or look at her like she was damaged. And couldn't he relate?

He was out of words. Completely out of his depth. Instead, he reached for her and she stepped into his careful embrace. Another display of trust.

After few seconds, she slid free. "Thanks." She cleared her throat. "I'm going to turn the news back on, but keep the volume off in case we get any more visitors."

"Good idea." End of discussion, but his mind churned. He poured himself more coffee while she found the remote and switched on the TV.

"Shit."

Kurt turned. "What's wrong?"

Her gaze never left the screen. "Glenn died."

According to the news, Glenn Lambert had succumbed to his injuries overnight.

I killed him. The words clanged in Caitlyn's head. Just hours ago, he'd taken his last breath, and it was her fault. He had been a vile man with murderous intentions, clearly complicit in his dad's crimes. He'd come at her with a knife. She couldn't regret her actions.

That didn't mean she was over it. She would have rather seen him face the justice and humiliation of a trial. Sadly, though, left to the court system, the entire Lambert family could easily go unpunished.

Not that she planned to hunt anyone down. Vigilante she was not.

As much as she wanted to be proactive about finding Rose, they needed more information. But they also couldn't stay sequestered in Brandon Marlowe's house forever. Nor did she want to be on the run from police and Lambert for the rest of her life. And she certainly couldn't subject Kurt to the same fate just for trying to help out a former friend.

Ever since she'd found Rose, Shaylee had been using her network to learn more about Lambert's company and dealings. Assuming Rose was okay—and Caitlyn couldn't bring herself to consider the alternative—they needed to find a way to get Rose out of his clutches and figure out if he was merely part of the organization behind the trafficking on St. Isidore, or he ran the business.

"Hey." Kurt appeared at her side. "Are you okay?"

She held her elbows and watched the silent newscaster as the story moved to ongoing cleanup efforts in the Leewards. "Why wouldn't I be?"

"Because no matter the circumstances, it's not easy to take a life."

"In this case, it should be." Her voice came out with an edge like chipped ice. "The world is better off without him." But he was still a person with a whole world inside his head, and family and friends who would mourn him, whether he deserved it or not.

She wouldn't cry over him, but that didn't mean she would throw a party either.

"If I were one of your guys, would you be worrying?" she asked.

"Yes. Absolutely." He crossed his arms, unconsciously mirroring her stance. "In fact, I have a plan for mental health services, and I encourage anyone on my team who needs them to use them. It's all confidential and I'll never know, but we need to reject the stigma behind people seeking help when they need it. It's hurting too many service members and civilians alike."

"You're a generous man." And like no one else she'd ever met.

He scoffed. "Also selfish. I want them to keep working for me and if they're messed up, they can't do their job."

Yeah, right. Was he afraid she'd think him a big softy? As if there was anything wrong with that. It only made her…*like* him more.

"Aren't we all a little messed up?"

His low laugh rumbled through her. "Yeah."

In retrospect, she probably should have sought counseling after Aaron attacked her. She'd thought herself so strong and tough, and he'd shattered that belief. Her physical wounds had healed, but she retreated into herself, hyperaware and skittish around men, hiding it under a hard shell of indifference and sarcasm.

She had spoken to Kurt as little as necessary and counted the days until he formally entered his PJ training and left Tinker for good. Having him around had been torture because he was everything she could want in a man, but he loathed her. And she was broken anyway, at the time not sure she'd ever want a man to touch her again.

And then she'd lost the baby. Kurt had noticed her car in the parking lot after hours and found her in the women's locker room, bleeding out on the floor. Part of her had hated him for seeing her at her most vulnerable. For caring for her while the paramedics were on their way. For making her realize how much she had lost by hurting him. For making her want more, the whole stupid fairy tale.

She had pushed him away even harder, refusing to see

him at the hospital, and then Terrell had brought her home and told her Kurt was gone. He'd been called up to start his training earlier than expected. No goodbye, just gone. Terrell had been the perfect friend then, no censure, no questions, just support.

That night she had cried for hours. When the tears were gone, she picked herself up and began the long process of putting herself back together, reclaiming control of her life, immersing herself in martial arts and self-defense classes that went far beyond the basic disarming and defensive techniques the Air Force had given her.

And, eventually, encounters with men who liked a woman who took charge had helped her heal and regain her confidence. But she could see now that Aaron had still stolen far too much from her.

She'd made herself too strong, her shell too hard, and Kurt had put cracks in her protective cover. If she let him get any closer she might shatter.

His large, warm hand enveloped hers, simultaneously filling her with a sense of calm and the desire to tug him closer. "I know you don't want to talk, but I'm here for you if you change your mind. Or just need a shoulder."

"Please, don't," she whispered, freeing her fingers from the comfort of his grasp.

"Okay." He straightened and put several inches between them. Not enough to reset her faulty inner compass that seemed calibrated to point to him. Nor enough to give her relief from his tantalizing scent. His expression was akin to someone who'd been sucker punched. "I didn't realize it bothered you," he said without a trace of irony, despite the fact that she'd practically wrapped herself around him less than an hour ago.

"I'm sorry," she said. "I just can't..." *Trust myself. Control myself. Let myself get attached.*

The combination of anger, hurt, and confusion on his handsome face made her chest ache.

"It's fine," he said, shifting away. "You don't owe me anything. And no one should ever touch you against your wishes."

Her wish was for him to continue what they'd started this morning. But what she needed was entirely different, so she merely watched him walk away.

The wait for stores on St. Isidore to open had been interminable. If Caitlyn had been willing, Kurt surely could have found an enjoyable way for them to pass the time. But after the morning's revelations, she'd retreated into pensive silence, playing solitaire with a deck of cards she found somewhere, and he couldn't blame her.

Instead, he'd wandered the house, periodically peeking through shutters for signs of surveillance, pulling books off the shelves, and watching the TV for news updates.

Finally, just before ten a.m., he checked the street for potential witnesses and, finding none, borrowed Marlowe's Land Rover and backed down the driveway. He wore the cricket cap and sunglasses with another pair of jammers and a T-shirt he'd purchased at the cruise terminal.

The computer store he'd found in the phone book was closed on Sundays, but he lucked out at a small variety shop next to a row of popular tourist restaurants. He grabbed two pay-as-you-go phones and a Wi-Fi enabled tablet marketed for kids.

An hour later he returned with the gadgets, a cheap pair of reading glasses—not strictly necessary unless he wanted to avoid a raging headache—enough food to hold them over for a few days, and changes of clothes for each of them, opting for dark colors in case they needed to sneak through the jungle again.

Within thirty minutes, Caitlyn had the phones programmed with all the important numbers, and Kurt had emailed Tara using a self-deleting email service Valerie had shown the team a couple years back. She and Tara were working through mounds of data about Lambert, Valerie digging up the info and Tara sorting through it while she worked.

The earliest any of his guys would be able to fly out was the next morning. With Caitlyn's approval, he asked Tara to purchase tickets for Jason and Dan on the first flight out.

Working through a VPN—virtual private network—that anonymized his location, Kurt checked his email, read the news, and scoured the maps of St. Isidore for…something. Did he really expect anything to jump out at him and scream, *Rose is here*?

"What else can I do?" Caitlyn asked, tapping her fingers on the counter.

All that restless energy and nowhere to put it. "I'll have Valerie post some of her findings where we can take a look at them. The more eyes the better, right?"

The tightness around Caitlyn's mouth relaxed a bit. "Thank you."

They spent the day sifting through Lambert's personal and business information, looking for something that might tell them where to find Rose, or something they could take to Shaylee's friend in the St. Isidore Royal Police Force that couldn't be ignored.

Needing a break, Kurt checked his email account. "Valerie sent another file drop," he said.

Caitlyn groaned. "I'm not wired to sit in front of a computer screen all day. A cockpit computer, yes, but this… I want to find something helpful, but right now I'm nothing but an oversized couch warmer."

Kurt started going through the files. "This is information on Lambert's finances that they've already gone through. He has a couple of shell corporations and what look like accounts with offshore banks that don't give out financial info."

Caitlyn stood and stretched and then parked next to his stool to peer over his shoulder, teasing him with her nearness.

Her rejection of his simple, gesture of support had cut deep, but none of this was about him. Not really. So he tried to let it roll off his back. Caitlyn was the one who'd been hurt.

He'd give her whatever she needed, even if it was space.

"What does that mean exactly?" she asked. "We already figured he had shady business dealings."

"Valerie managed to track payments from the so-called employers of some of the people The Underground has helped rescue. The evidence isn't probably legal in any court of law, but it shows a direct link between Lambert's corporate holdings—"

"And the trafficking victims. You're saying he's not just a customer, he's a supplier?"

"Looks like it," he said, satisfaction evident in his voice.

"Well, that's something." Caitlyn sat back with a thoughtful frown.

Knowing Lambert was in on the whole scheme raised the stakes, and put Rose in greater danger if he knew that she'd been working undercover.

"Can't this help us narrow down possible locations for where he's keeping Rose? This sitting around is killing me. We need to find her ASAP."

Assuming Lambert had her at all. And that he hadn't

killed her already. *Fuck.* Kurt would definitely not be sharing *that* thought.

"Valerie is looking at Lambert's contacts and trying to track his location. Anything you know that we don't might help." Without some solid piece of intel to act upon, there wasn't much they could do. Short of driving around the island randomly hoping to spot her... Talk about impossible. "I understand how you're feeling, but we need something to point us in the right direction, otherwise we're useless. We can't go off half-cocked with nothing."

She let out a heavy sigh. And rubbed her forehead. "I know. I know. I'm just frustrated. And worried."

"I get it." He sat on his hands so he wouldn't do something stupid.

A message from Tara popped up. *Check your work email.*

He navigated to the portal for his official email, which Tara regularly skimmed, cleaning things up and pointing out important correspondence, just as she did with the snail mail. The third message from the top was from a sender he didn't recognize, but more importantly the subject was ROSE.

> *We have Rose. Will trade her for Caitlyn Brevard and Kurt Steele. No police. No backup.*
> *More details after response.*

"She's still alive," Caitlyn said on a relieved breath.

The attached image showed Rose standing in front of a clock tower at a cruise ship terminal, holding today's newspaper. The shadows were long and the clock showed four-thirty. The message had been sent a few minutes after five o'clock.

"That's the port in Sancoins," Caitlyn said.

"I'm replying 'yes,'" Kurt said. "I'll see if Valerie can trace that email." That might even be what Lambert was attempting to do in reverse. He looked to her, realizing he'd gone into boss mode. "I assume that's what you want."

"Of course."

He sent the reply and stared at the screen. The clock on the kitchen wall ticked loudly, suddenly the most obnoxious thing Kurt had ever heard, and he hadn't even noticed it until now. Caitlyn seemed to be holding her breath as she paced the living room. Everything in him screamed to go to her, but he wouldn't make that mistake twice.

They waited in silence, unable to do anything. Which was stupid. It could take hours, hell, even overnight, for them to hear—

A new message popped into his Inbox.

CHAPTER ELEVEN

"I HAVE A REPLY," KURT said from his perch at the counter.

Caitlyn's stomach jumped. "What is it?" She jogged to his side.

"Brevard and Steele only. Six a.m. Whiffle Beach gazebo. Follow these rules or the sister dies."

An anguished sound escaped her throat. *Oh, Rose.* She shook off the suffocating vine of helplessness creeping over her and found her voice. "Whiffle Beach is closed to the public for repairs to the boardwalk and facilities, so it'll be deserted. I know they won't willingly let any of us live, but you have to tell them yes. Absolutely yes."

"The storm means we won't have any backup."

"I know."

"Okay." He sent the reply.

Kurt stared at his screen. "You know it's a trap."

"Yes, but what choice do we have?"

"None."

"You don't have to go," she said, surprised by how much she liked having someone with her to face this ordeal. Having him around made it easier. Half of her wanted him with her to face down the enemy. The other half wanted him safely on the other side of the world. "She's my sister. This is my fight."

His mouth twisted into a scowl. "If you think I would walk away now, then you don't know me at all."

"No." She never doubted he'd stay. "But I had to offer."

"Whatever."

She'd offended his pride, but she wouldn't apologize. She removed the engagement ring from her finger and made reflected light play in patterns across the granite. "Somehow they know she's my sister."

"All it would take is a little digging. Or that woman on the stairs might have talked."

Probably against her will.

Tears burned the back of Caitlyn's eyes and her throat tightened. A stupid, useless response. She slid the ring across the counter until it struck the wall with a faint *clink*.

"Hey," Kurt said.

Without responding, she crossed the room and ran up the stairs.

She shut the door to her room and sat on the bed, breathing deeply until she regained control. Out the window, the palm trees waved their arms wildly in the offshore breeze, looking far too exuberant.

Somewhere out there in the fading daylight, Rose was alive, thank God. But Caitlyn didn't trust Lambert or his goons an inch. Surely her sister was being used as bait to get Caitlyn and Kurt to show up so Lambert could take his revenge on his son's killer and get rid of all the witnesses to Rose's captivity.

But he wasn't a dumb man. Would he hunt down everyone at Steele? Their families? How far would he go, and how many people would he endanger?

She couldn't let that happen. No matter what went down in the morning, whether she and Kurt survived, they needed to rescue Rose, and take down Lambert before he could hurt anyone else.

She didn't know how to do that yet. All they had was the gun Kurt had grabbed from Glenn's partner last night.

Why had she left Glenn's weapon behind after she'd shot him?

That now-familiar sick feeling doused her like a cold shower.

Breathe.

Heavily guarded as Lambert was, he would be hard to pin down. Not to mention, he had the local police in his pocket and public opinion on his side.

Caitlyn paced, the floorboards squeaking beneath her feet. They were meeting at Whiffle Beach at six a.m. It wasn't even six *p.m.* yet. *Christ.* She would not survive the wait without a distraction.

No way could she sleep. She needed something to do, something to feel productive. If only they had access to weapons and a range for target practice. At least then she would be able get out some of her aggression and feel like she was doing something proactive that might help tomorrow.

Lambert couldn't possibly expect her and Kurt to show up unarmed.

God, *Kurt.* If she thought turning herself over to Lambert alone would protect Kurt and his family and friends, she'd do it now. She couldn't live with him getting hurt or killed.

Though chances were she wouldn't have to live with it. She'd probably be dead in less than twenty-four hours.

To prevent that from happening, she had to stop fretting

about everyone else and focus.

"Where are you, Rose?"

Forcing her leaden body to move, she returned downstairs. Kurt stood at the counter spreading peanut butter and jelly on bread.

Before he could start throwing out suggestions about how to handle the message from Lambert, she said, "If there's any way we can find her, I think we need to hit first, tonight."

"I agree. And it turns out we might be able to."

Her shoulders relaxed a fraction. Dare she hope? "How's that?"

"I was about to come get you. Valerie was able to trace the IP address of the email. Believe it or not, it was sent from St. Isidore."

"Wouldn't we expect that?" Caitlyn asked. It made sense that Lambert's men would be holding Rose close by if they were going to bring her to the exchange tomorrow.

"Yes, but not if they were masking their location. If they were using an anonymizing browser or a virtual private network, it wouldn't have traced back directly to the island. It might've looked like it was coming from somewhere like the Netherlands or Russia or Chicago." He gave a little head tilt. "According to Valerie."

"So if they're not masking their location, can we narrow it down to an area more precise than the island?"

Little red indentations from Kurt's glasses sat on the bridge of his nose. "Yes. She was able to do just that, and it looks like they're on the northwest side of the island. It's not definitive, she can't pinpoint their location like GPS, but she can get within a mile or less. Something to do with local routers or something, I don't know. But Tara thought to narrow it down by looking at properties or known connections that Lambert has on that end of St. Iz, based on the financial info Valerie put together."

Damn. Kurt had amazing people on his team. As much as Caitlyn hated getting him involved, where would she be without Steele's resources? She'd have little or nothing to go on right now. Or she'd already be behind bars.

Or worse.

"Assuming they're operating somewhere nearby and haven't moved," Kurt said, "she found two possibilities. One is Zanana Shores, a resort that's currently under renovation, located on an isolated spit of land at the top of Zanana Bay, just north of Terre Verte. According to what Valerie dug up, Lambert purchased Zanana two years ago after the economy started to improve, and it's set to open next month.

"The other is a private home that belongs to the Devaux family, who appear to be beneficiaries of Lambert's cheap labor."

Caitlyn couldn't stop her lip from curling. What was wrong with people?

"The resort seems like a perfect place to stage trafficking victims," Kurt said. "If there's a dock, it would be simple to bring them in via boat from other islands, and St. Isidore's minimal coast guard presence doesn't present much threat. If done right, no one would notice the new faces among the resort's tourists. There are also a couple of airfields near TV that would make it easy for them to come and go."

Against her will, hope lodged itself in Caitlyn's heart like an axe into wood. "The hotel makes more sense, right? It's isolated and not open yet, so there's less risk of Lambert's men being spotted with Rose." She mentally swiped away imagined scenes of Rose struggling with her captors. Going down that path was immobilizing.

"I agree," Kurt said. "Plus I messaged Dan and Jason.

They confirmed that north of TV, the island is pretty quiet. Lambert's men would likely see it as more difficult for Rose to escape from. I'd put my money there too."

Kurt threw a concerned look Caitlyn's way. "If we had backup, I'd send someone to the house too, but we'll have to make it our Plan B instead."

"And if she's not at either one…"

Kurt's somber midnight gaze held hers. "We go to the exchange at six."

For dinner, Kurt heated canned stew in a pot while Caitlyn sliced a loaf of French bread. With a little olive oil and vinegar on the side for dipping, the meal was almost first-class.

They ate to the sound of spoons clinking on ceramic bowls, the air in the room taut. Next to him, she tapped her toe on the stool's footrest as if trying to drive the nervous energy from her body. Her shoulders were so tense they nearly touched her ears.

He was almost as tightly wound. Everything hinged on tonight.

After they finished eating and washed the dishes, Caitlyn set out a small package she found in the cupboard. "How about dessert?"

"What are they?" Kurt asked.

"Coconut Shirley biscuits. Cookies. They're a Barbados staple."

"I thought you felt bad eating Brandon Marlowe's food."

"They'll go stale before he gets back." She gave him a wily cat's smile and shrugged. "I figure if we finish them off, we're doing him a favor."

More likely, she needed something that felt good, even if it was just a sugar hit. Kurt couldn't blame her.

While eating, they hashed out rough plans of attack and retreat for all the scenarios, drawing crude maps on paper taken from the printer in the study. They were undermanned, under-informed, and under-equipped, but they had little choice in such a short time frame.

He wished he could force her to stay behind. If anything happened to her, he would suffer the rest of his life. Short-lived though it might be.

He sighed.

This was ludicrous. For a man who claimed to want a family, he hadn't done much to make it happen over the last few years. Instead, he'd poured all his energy into Steele and compared every woman he met to Caitlyn.

Would he like to have children? Yes. But given a choice between having a family with another woman and spending his life with Caitlyn alone... He hadn't been lying when he told her that finding the right woman was far more important. If she'd take him, he would jettison the dream of a family, no regrets.

He stretched his arms overhead and stood, suddenly restless.

Across the counter from him, she stared at their plans and fiddled with a pen. She was beautiful, smart, fierce, and so precious now that the thought of losing her was nauseating.

And maybe it was about time she knew that. Whether she returned his feelings or not—and at this point he was pretty sure she didn't—he didn't want them to face this danger without her knowing she was loved.

The word carved a hollow in his chest, but it was the right one. "Love" had never applied to any other woman in his life. Not this kind of love, anyway.

Caitlyn leaned her elbows against the breakfast bar, her

brilliant green eyes subdued as she stared at a spot on the wall.

"If Rose is there, we'll get her," Kurt said.

She met his gaze, her eyes lighting with intensity. "I know."

He cleared his throat. "Can we talk for a minute?"

A crease formed between her brows. They were already talking, weren't they? And he was an idiot.

"Of course," she said, striding around the breakfast bar to join him in the great room. "What's up?"

He leaned against the side of the sofa and crossed his arms. Was he making a mistake? Shit. This was the dumbest idea ever. He wracked his brain for an alternate topic that might fit his change of tone.

"Kurt?" She stood in front of him with her hands on her hips and leaned over to move into his line of sight. "Everything all right?"

He straightened, took a deep breath, and looked her in the eyes. "I love you."

CHAPTER TWELVE

KURT GRIMACED AS THE WORDS escaped his mouth, seemingly against his will. Caitlyn's jaw slackened. Had he really just said—

"I know you don't feel the same, and that you don't want me to touch you now that we're not pretending to be engaged anymore, but in case something happens to me tomorrow…" He took a deep breath. "I just wanted you to know. That I love you. Pretty sure I always have."

Always? Like fourteen years always?

He'd knocked the breath right out of her, but his words didn't instill the deep terror she had expected.

Hell, she was vulnerable to him whether she pushed him away or not. Why was she running so hard from what she wanted? Had she been happier alone all these years? Had keeping her distance from those who threatened her heart made the important people in her life any less of an Achilles heel for her? No. He had the power to hurt her even if they never kissed again.

"That's all I had to say," he said, filling the heavy silence with his rich voice. "No expectations or anything, no matter how this all turns out." He shifted away from the couch and dropped his arms.

"Don't leave," she said, finally finding her voice as she reached out and laid her palm flat against his chest.

He went perfectly still except for the steady thump of his heart beneath her hand.

She inhaled his heady masculine scent and cleared her throat. "I don't know about love. I've avoided that my whole adult life." She placed her other hand on his chest and slid them both across to his massive biceps. "I've also avoided anyone who makes me feel...vulnerable."

His inky eyes never left hers.

"For example, you," she said. There. Maybe she wasn't such a coward after all. He'd humbled himself before her; the least she could do was be honest in return.

"*Me?*" His eyebrows crashed together. "Do I intimidate you?"

She shook her head. How to explain? "No. I mean you're obviously bigger and stronger, but I'm not talking about physical strength." Placing one hand on her heart, she whispered, "You make me vulnerable here."

His chin pulled back. "And you hate that."

How did he know her so well? "More than anything. If I don't let anyone get too close, they can't hurt me."

He placed his hand over hers on her chest, prodding her pulse. "That's a lonely way to live."

It was. It had been. "For a long time, I thought it was worth it. But all my best efforts have failed. I'm still here at Lambert's bidding to save my sister, because she's part of my family. How could I not be? And I'd still do anything to keep you safe, because we're friends and I...care."

His eyes flickered—possibly with disappointment—but

she couldn't tell him she loved him. She didn't know if the flutter in her belly and the vise around her heart were from love or fear. Or both. But, oh, how she wanted him.

Tonight could be their last chance. And if something happened to her, she didn't want his last memories of them together to be of her pushing him away. Not when she wanted to touch him more than anything. Besides, if she didn't live past the morning, it wouldn't matter how defenseless he made her feel.

Right now, she wanted to give in to the flame of desire that he lit within her. She wanted to truly live without any care for the wreck she might become if she fell under his spell. She glanced at his lips, unable to stop herself from giving away her goal.

His breath ceased and his gaze held as she slowly leaned in, compelled closer, as if he had his own gravity. Her skin tingled, the air turning warm between them.

She closed her eyes and pressed her mouth to his soft lips.

Every cell in her body sighed at the rightness of it. Every nerve sprang to life at the contact. She buzzed as if electrified and wrapped her arms around his neck to pull him close.

A low groan escaped him as their bodies met from shoulders to thighs. He deepened the kiss, tongues stroking and dueling, fanning the spark into an inferno. He tasted of desire and coconut. She wanted to strip them both naked and

—

"Hang on." She pulled back.

He frowned, but didn't say anything. Or move.

"Sit," she said, pointing to the couch. Would he let her take the reins?

She removed her T-shirt.

His frown vanished. He watched her with a hungry

expression as he settled onto the cushions, palms flat at his sides, appearing willing to go along with whatever she had in mind.

She approached him slowly, shedding her bra along the way. A low groan issued from his lips as he followed her progress, eyes unblinking, pupils flared. The look on his face was intoxicating.

The power of baring herself to this man, body and soul, surged through her veins, a high even better than cruising at twenty thousand feet. It made no sense, but no way in hell was she going to stop.

As she neared the sofa, she kicked off her running shoes and dropped her jeans and panties.

"Caitlyn, Jesus." Kurt gripped the front edge of the cushion, his knuckles white, his voice hoarse.

She smiled and lowered herself gently onto his lap. "Is this okay?" The edge of his sockets pressed against the backs of her thighs, but not painfully. She was more concerned about hurting him.

His hips twitched at the contact. "Hell, yeah."

She kissed him, melting into his warm body, threading her hands into his short hair. He responded eagerly but kept his arms at his sides even as his pelvis rocked against hers.

Pulling back, she held his rough cheeks. "What's wrong?"

"Not a goddamned thing."

"Why won't you touch me?"

He glanced between them and chuckled. "I'm pretty sure this counts."

"Kurt." She rolled her hips and his eyes glazed. "I take back what I said earlier. I thought that was obvious."

"Sure." He shrugged, his eyes never leaving her face. "I'm just giving you full control."

Tears—for God's sake, *tears*—burned at the backs of her

eyes.

Fuck that.

She kissed him hard and grabbed his hands, placing them on her breasts.

He smiled into the kiss and murmured, "Yes, ma'am," against her lips. Then he caressed her eager flesh as his mouth moved lower, trailing sparks down her neck and along her shoulder.

Head thrown back, she arched into him and gave a lusty moan, her body more fully alive than she'd ever imagined possible. His lips scorched across her skin like a brushfire. When his mouth closed over her nipple, she nearly jumped out of his lap.

He thought he was *giving* her control? More like unraveling it.

And she couldn't care less.

As he caressed and teased, she reached between them to unbutton his pants and slip her hand into his boxers. He hissed at her touch, but didn't stop driving her mad with his clever tongue.

His penis was smooth and warm, pulsing in her hand as she stroked. He let his head drop back with a groan, but continued caressing and exploring with his hands, moving lower until he found the sensitive spot between her thighs.

Her body spooled up like a propeller, gaining momentum as he touched her with expert fingers. Their breath filled the air, hot gasps, desperate sighs, and hushed moans as they drove each other higher, undulating together in an ancient rhythm.

Sweat pebbled on Caitlyn's skin. She flushed hot and cold as she raced toward the sweet reward promised in Kurt's every touch.

Her breath stopped and she turned weightless, catapulted

into the stars as he brought her to ecstasy.

The force of it left her speechless. And eager for more. Still buzzing, she rose onto her knees and guided him between her thighs, sliding down until he was buried deep.

"Ah, God." His low voice rumbled through her. He gripped her hips and set a steady pace that drove her wild.

Watching Kurt come undone was almost as intoxicating as his touch.

"*Caitlyn*." He went rigid and stopped moving, releasing a groan of pure anguish. "No condom."

"I'm clean," she said, quickly. "It's been years."

His dark eyes widened. "Me too, but—"

She should have covered this earlier, but it wasn't exactly sexy foreplay. Of course, having the talk now certainly wasn't a mood enhancer. "I can't have kids. I had to have a hysterectomy after…"

"Oh, shit, Cait. I'm sorry." He stroked her face.

"It's okay." She gave him a quick kiss to clear his furrowed brow. "Really. It's been twelve years. And I never wanted kids anyway, so…" She'd never had that maternal urge that so many women seemed to get, not before her miscarriage and not since. If she had, she could have adopted. There were plenty of orphans in need. "I'm fine."

The temperature of the air between them had dropped, and their breathing returned to normal. And here she sat naked on a fully dressed man whose ardor was quickly cooling.

Kurt stared into the dim room beyond her shoulder. Was he disappointed that she couldn't have children, or just lost in the memory of that awful night when he'd probably saved her life?

"There's nothing you could have done to change that outcome," she said.

His startled gaze met hers. He shouldn't be so surprised. She knew how his brain worked. At least when it came to rescuing people.

"There is something you could do now, though." She slid a foot between the back cushion and his buttocks, and used her calf to press him all the way inside her, covering his face in soft kisses until he grasped her cheeks and fused their mouths together for a desperate, hungry exploration of lips, teeth, and tongues.

"Please," she whispered. "Please love me."

With a grunt, he wrapped his arms across her upper back and held her shoulders, driving into her over and over until she was delirious, his hot breath tickling her neck.

Within moments, he lost his rhythm, his thrusts coming hard and fast. Reaching between them, he stroked her with his thumb as he came inside her with a long, shuddering sigh.

Tensing, she held her breath, closed her eyes, and followed him into oblivion.

Kurt didn't want to move. Where else would he want to be but buried in this woman whose limbs swaddled him, inhaling the sweet scent of her neck, his hands full of her smooth skin?

They'd gone from "don't touch me" to "don't stop" in the space of a few hours, and he was still reeling.

The soft hum of the air conditioner kicking on preceded a blast of cool air from overhead. Goosebumps spread across Caitlyn's back and she shivered.

He raised his head and she opened her glittering green eyes to look at him, her saucy grin sending a little thrill through him.

"Thank you," she said, her voice husky as she leaned in for a quick kiss.

"For what?"

She rolled her eyes.

He chuckled. "I mean if there was something specific, I'd like to know so I can be sure to do it again."

Sobering, she combed her fingers through the hair above his ears, a move that made it impossible to think. "I wish we had the time," she said, gracing him with a soft kiss.

Gradually, her words sank in, slapping him across the face. According to his watch it was just after eight and fully dark outside. "Shit. We have to move out in thirty."

And he needed to clean up. Ideally, he would take a break from wearing his artificial legs too, but for one night, he could deal with it. He'd charged them up the day before, so he should be fine.

Before he could rethink his reaction to the time and revel further in Caitlyn's embrace, she had jumped off his lap and donned her underwear. "Hey, I didn't mean—"

"It's okay." She stooped to picked up her shirt and walked toward the coffee table under which her bra had landed. "You said it yourself. We need to get moving."

He tried to ignore the bitter taste in his mouth. His heart was fragile after his confession, and the sense of déjà vu from the few sexual encounters since his amputation was not serving him well. He snatched a tissue from a box on the end table and cleaned up best he could, then hastily tucked himself into his pants.

Caitlyn fastened her bra and slid her shirt over her head, hiding all the beautiful skin he'd hardly had a chance to explore.

"Okay." Standing, he straightened his clothes and ran a hand through his hair. Why hadn't he at least removed his shirt so he could feel her naked breasts against his chest when he had the chance?

With a sigh, she slid on her running shoes and kneeled to tie the laces, but toyed with them instead. "I don't know how to do this."

"What, the two minutes after?"

Her short laugh carried little humor. "Pretty much." She sat on the floor with her elbows on her knees and rested her forehead on her fingertips. "I don't know how to think beyond this…event. To be honest, I'm not sure I'll ever be able to."

Well, how was that for a knife to the chest? "Hey, you don't have to. We didn't make any promises."

"I know." She tied her shoes and stood. "But after what you said…"

"That I love you?" He was done tiptoeing around it.

She nodded and held one arm across her ribs, her focus on his chin.

A boulder lodged in his stomach. "If that was some kind of pity fuck because you can't return my feelings—"

"*No.*" She finally looked him in the eye. "No." Tentatively, she clasped his face between her hands. "I've wanted you since the day I walked into your office two weeks ago."

Not nearly as long as he'd wanted her, but did that really matter? His chest eased a little, and the dark freckle that straddled the edge of her upper lip the way she'd straddled his lap just moments before snagged his attention.

He wanted to lick that mesmerizing dot of color.

She kissed him.

Before he could even get an arm around her waist, it was over and she was backing away with a subdued smile. "I like you, Kurt. And I really like kissing you and everything."

"*I* like where this is headed."

She laughed. "We need to get moving, remember?"

This time he kissed her, hard. "Be safe tonight, okay?"

"You too, Superman." She gave him another quick peck on the lips and left the room.

It wasn't "I love you," but he'd take it.

By ten-thirty, Caitlyn and Kurt were less than half a mile from Zanana Shores, which took its name from the local word for pineapple.

They had left Brandon Marlowe's Land Rover in a dirt pullout that locals and plugged-in tourists used for easy access to the beaches along Zanana Bay. The sliver of moon low in the sky and the thick spatter of stars overhead offered little light, and the jungle was black as tar.

Keeping her focus on the faint line that marked the edge of the asphalt, Caitlyn trod softly on the sandy shoulder in Kurt's wake, headed for the pair of lights up ahead that flanked the entrance to the resort.

Without night-vision equipment—and with no help from the moon—they couldn't risk using the jungle for cover. There were too many hazards, and using flashlights was out of the question.

The road was more exposed but they could move faster.

She tried to block out thoughts of anything else but their surroundings. Thinking about Rose made her restless.

Memories of making love to Kurt had the same effect, though decidedly more pleasant. Sex with someone she truly cared for had been incredible. Mind-blowingly better than anything she'd ever experienced.

Scary.

And absolutely the last thing she needed right now.

But the feel of his hands and mouth on her skin, loving her, moving inside her…

Gah. Stop it.

She pulled herself back to the moment. The noise of the

bugs and frogs, the air thick in her lungs, the rustle of the leaves on the breeze. Kurt's broad back.

He may have transitioned to a desk job, but the need to jump into the fray to protect and save seethed under his skin. He still had the aura of a deadly weapon honed to a fine point.

Yet, he could be so gentle.

And he loved her.

Was that why he'd agreed to help her from the start? And, God, if he'd truly always loved her—as he'd claimed earlier—no wonder he'd taken her rejection so hard. Had he pulled out of her life without a goodbye and thrown himself into PJ training as a form of protection?

Her throat tightened. She understood that as well as anyone.

About a hundred yards from the freshly stuccoed wall that marked the entrance to Zanana Shores, Kurt held up a hand and stopped walking. She barely managed not to collide with him.

Up ahead at the gate, two guards stood on the side of the road, lazily holding rifles and chatting.

Kurt pointed to his left, and they veered into the vegetation just enough to be hidden from the road while using the light from the street lamps to avoid tripping on tree roots or holes in the ground.

Snakes she wouldn't even think about. St. Isidore had a few nasty ones.

Caitlyn's heart knocked into her ribs with more force the closer they got. *Please let Rose be here.*

They had studied the layout of the resort from an aerial map Valerie had found, but had no idea how many of Lambert's men were guarding the compound. For all they knew, this whole thing was a trap.

No fence encircled the hotel grounds, so they crept past the wall, which bore a sea-themed tile mosaic embedded with the resort's name. So far, they hadn't seen a soul other than the sentries, but as they approached the open-air reception building that formed the right-hand terminus of the upside-down-V-shaped string of cabins, low, deep voices stirred the quiet.

Caitlyn grabbed Kurt's arm to keep herself from running straight toward the sound. He gave her the signal to duck down. They doubled over and jogged toward the first villa, where dim light glimmered around the edges of thick curtains that hung in the front window.

Slipping between the cabin and the pool house, they came out on the beach side, suddenly assaulted by a stiff wind, and the shushing sounds of the ocean not a hundred yards from the back patios that lined the spit of land to give each guest a view of either the Caribbean Sea or Zanana Bay.

Vine-covered trellises on either side of the patios provided a measure of privacy between villas, and shielded Caitlyn and Kurt from view.

Bending at the waist, both of them peered through the slats and the glass sliding door beyond, which had no curtains or blinds. Five men appeared to be sleeping on thick piles of blankets spread around the tile floor.

She didn't recognize any of them, nor the two who sat on folding chairs hunched over a small table playing cards, guns on the table. What she guessed was the bathroom was dark beyond the open door.

No sign of Rose.

They went down the line, finding three more rooms with a similar setup. In one cabin lit only with a nightlight, nine women huddled together in a dark corner—none of them Rose—watched over by two guards.

"The big, white guy is Jack Cartwright," she whispered into Kurt's ear. The other she didn't know.

They moved swiftly down the line. All of the rooms beyond the apex of the V, facing the bay, were dark and devoid of people, but fully furnished and ready for guests.

The pool house was also empty.

"She's not here." Caitlyn had known this was a gamble, but she couldn't ignore the leaden feeling in her chest.

Kurt grasped her hand and whispered, "We'll find her."

"We have to do something about the people who are trapped here."

"Call Shaylee. Have her call her police friend. Then we can check the other buildings. Maybe Rose is in one of them."

Caitlyn quickly made the call, giving Shaylee all the information they had. Somehow, Rose's girlfriend held it together. Probably the same way Caitlyn was right now. Sheer will.

Shaylee had no idea how long it would take for her friend to mobilize a team she could trust. For now, they were on their own.

Caitlyn and Kurt jogged in a straight line from the tip of one wing to the other. The only buildings they hadn't yet explored were the reception center, the restaurant, and the equipment rental shed.

So far they had encountered no perimeter security other than the guards at the front gate, who were probably there to prevent looters and squatters who might stumble upon the operation. Given the setup, Lambert seemed more worried about people escaping.

She and Kurt quickly cleared the areas behind the check-in desk, the tours office, management offices, and housekeeping. The gift shop was stuffed full of unopened boxes, its door locked, no sign of anyone inside.

If her sister wasn't here—

"Not another step."

Caitlyn knew that voice, that Aussie accent. She turned. With a rifle pointed at her chest, she'd never reach the knife tucked into her bra before he shot her. She held up her hands. "Hello, Jack."

CHAPTER THIRTEEN

FUCK. KURT TURNED TO FACE the big man pointing an AK-47 at them. He'd been scanning their surroundings, watching for guards, but he wasn't omniscient. And now Caitlyn was in greater danger than before.

"Drop your weapon," the other man said, jerking his chin toward the Sig in Kurt's hand.

Kurt laid the gun gently on the ground.

"Glenn died," Cartwright said, his dark eyes glittery with anger in the lights from the pool deck.

"I know," Caitlyn said, her voice soft. "I never wished that for him."

The big man took a step closer. "Then maybe you shouldn't have shot him. "

She said nothing.

Cartwright frowned and used his free hand to talk into his radio. "Christophe, we have visitors. I'm bringing them your way."

They needed a way to distract this Hulk so they could run for it. Then again, if Rose were here, they couldn't leave her behind.

"Couldn't wait until six o'clock, eh?"

Caitlyn straightened. "Where is she?"

Cartwright's mouth curled into a nasty grin and he waved them toward the stairs to the pool. "Lead on."

Kurt could almost feel the hope radiating off Caitlyn, despite the dire situation.

When they reached the stairs, he let her descend ahead of him, then he gripped the rail and took his time going step over step. He had mastered stairs years ago, but that didn't mean he could race down them.

The big man followed closely on his heels, prodding him impatiently with the barrel of his rifle. Kurt sped up slightly, then stopped abruptly and bent over.

Cartwright barreled into him and they both fell down the remaining few steps onto the pool deck. The Aussie reached for the rifle, but Caitlyn kicked it away. He gripped Kurt's leg, tugging hard, as if trying to pull off his prosthesis. Instead he threatened to dislocate Kurt's hip.

Caitlyn kicked the Hulk in the head, and then dove for the rifle. Cartwright grabbed her ankle with his other hand and she went down, kicking at his face until he let go. Kurt levered himself up to sitting and slammed their attacker on the nose with the heel of his hand. The man howled but didn't release him, dragging Kurt across the rough ground as he rolled away.

Kurt angled for a better position to strike, punching the man's biceps with a sharp stab of his knuckles.

His grip loosened and Kurt pushed onto his knees, grabbing the rifle and swiveling to face the Hulk, who now held Caitlyn down with both hands, even as she thrashed.

"Let her go," Kurt said, aiming the weapon at Cartwright's chest.

The man released her, and Caitlyn scrambled to her feet.

"Where's Rose?" she asked, her voice steady, sharp as a razor.

"Fuck you."

"You said it yourself. I killed Glenn. What makes you think we would hesitate to do the same to you?"

Kurt tried to expand his peripheral vision. There had to be a rope or cord lying around that she could use to secure the brute. Had the hotel stocked the lifesaver yet?

Something flashed in the dark to their right. More people. "Shit. Cait, we have to move."

She shot a look over her shoulder and then nodded.

He handed her the rifle, which she kept trained on Cartwright, and Kurt straightened both legs, walking his hands toward his feet to push himself up until he could stand. Sidling toward the stairs, Caitlyn paralleled him from the other side of the giant, who still sat on the ground. Once up the steps, they took off running.

He glanced back. Cartwright was on his knees holding his bloody nose, waving his team in Kurt and Caitlyn's direction.

Armed men on their heels, they burst through the opening at the north end of the building and came face-to-face with a wall of men holding rifles.

Footsteps echoed behind them, neatly cutting off their escape.

They all stood and waited, breathing hard.

"Drop it," said a tall, thin man with skin the color of a walnut, his hair in short cornrows.

Caitlyn set the AK gently at her feet and nudged it in the lanky man's direction.

"How nice to see another familiar face, Christophe," she said.

The man's expression remained stony and his aim did not

waver.

If Kurt and Caitlyn could coordinate it so that they dropped at the same time, all these men might shoot each other. But it was too risky. He wasn't willing to get Caitlyn killed, and despite his nickname, he was no superhero who could take on eight men at once and expect to survive.

Cartwright lumbered into view, his lips and chin bloody, nose red and swollen. He glared at Kurt, but didn't approach him. "You want to see Rose? Then let's go."

So they'd guessed right. Small consolation.

"Pat them down," the Aussie said to one of the men next to Christophe.

Before leaving the house, Kurt had considered stuffing one of Marlowe's steak knives in his waistband as a backup, but figured without a sheath, he'd probably just stab himself in the gut. So this lackey would find him unarmed.

They were patted down before being marched along a paved path to the rental equipment shed. Christophe and his men entered first, the bright light from inside spilling out into the darkness. Kurt and Caitlyn entered next, followed by three more men with guns, and the Hulk.

In the far corner of the high-ceilinged-but-empty wooden building, a woman with bronze skin and springy red hair floating in a cloud around her face sat in a plastic chair, arms behind her back. At the commotion, she looked up and her dark eyes widened. "Caity?"

"Rose!" Caitlyn rushed forward and wrapped her arms around her sister, murmuring words that Kurt couldn't hear.

"*Enough.*" Christophe crossed the small room and grabbed Caitlyn's hair, jerking her away from the other woman so hard that she stumbled.

If his hands were free, Kurt would've beaten the man into a bloody mess. The last time he'd been this helpless was when he awoke in a hospital without his legs six years ago. Or maybe when Caitlyn had told him about Aaron.

Fuck.

He and Caitlyn were placed in separate corners—him to Rose's right and Caitlyn diagonally across from her—and tied to their chairs. The men left the room, leaving behind only Christophe and another black man who was short and stout, his head bald.

"You start outside," Christophe said. "I've got this."

His teammate left, shutting the door behind him and locking it with an audible *click*.

"I'm so sorry," Caitlyn said to her sister, ignoring the presence of their jailer. "We were trying to save you."

"You never should have come." A tear tracked down her face. "I'm sorry I got you into this."

"We looked for you at the party."

Rose scowled. "A couple days after that morning you showed up at the house, I tried to run, but the guards caught me." Her gaze dropped and her lips disappeared between her teeth. "I ended up in a clinic for a week, and then I... I stayed in Glenn's condo until they brought me here."

Stayed? She made it sound like she'd had a choice, but clearly that wasn't the case. Kurt tried to unclench his jaw. What had these assholes done to her?

"No more talking," their guard said, "or I will gag you."

"Christophe."

He scowled at Caitlyn and approached her chair. "What?"

"What are we doing here? What are we waiting for?"

Was she trying to get him to kill her?

Christophe glared at her for a moment, and then said, "We are waiting for Mr. Lambert. He has been looking for you, and he will decide how to clean up this mess."

"How long?"

Christophe's eyes narrowed and he shrugged. "It could be minutes or hours."

So much for helpful information, but she had been smart to try.

"Can we get some water?" she asked.

"No." He sat in his chair near the door and glowered. "No more talking."

For the first few minutes, he kept a close eye on them, but eventually he pulled out his cell phone and began thumbing the screen. Caitlyn and her sister stared at each other. Their similarities ended with hair color and freckles. Caitlyn had a tall, athletic physique, while Rose was short and curvy. Both were beautiful in their own way. Both were willing to risk their lives to save others.

Both deserved to make it out of here alive.

Some unreadable expression passed between the sisters, and Caitlyn surreptitiously focused her attention on Christophe, appearing to stare at the floor while periodically glancing up through her lashes at the guard.

The bored sentry occasionally scanned the room, as if to ensure they hadn't moved, but he seemed unconcerned given that their hands were bound and tied to their seats. Rose rocked in her chair, and Caitlyn coughed several times, drawing the guard's gaze. Clamping her mouth shut, she tucked her chin to her chest as if trying to muffle the sound.

Christophe's attention returned to his phone.

Caitlyn glanced at Rose, who tipped her head the barest fraction and slowly blinked, flattening her lips in concentration. Out of the corner of his eye, Kurt saw a silver flash from behind Rose's back. A knife? He looked at Caitlyn. She held his gaze, her eyes intelligent and fierce, and gave him the barest hint of a smile.

If he hadn't been in love with her before, he was ass over

teakettle now.

Some time later—but still dark through the small gaps in the wooden walls—Caitlyn jolted awake at the sound of her sister's cries of pain. Her heart played drum major against her sternum. "What's the matter? What's going on?"

Rose didn't look up, but thank God, she wasn't under attack. Was this part of her plan? Caitlyn blinked to clear her head and glanced at Kurt, who appeared alert, his eyes tracking their captor.

Christophe stood and stowed his phone, hands on his weapon, eyes wide and wary, his pace measured as he approached Rose. "What the fuck is wrong with you?"

Rose's upper body curled in, like she would double over if she weren't tied to the chair. "I don't know," she said, her voice a taut and screechy mimic of a poorly played violin. "My stomach." Air hissed through her teeth. "I think it might be the baby."

Caitlyn pulsed with shock like a struck gong.

"Baby?" Christophe frowned and took a step back, examining her as if he could diagnose her with his eyes. "You're pregnant?"

Caitlyn ignored Kurt's palpable gaze, her heart rate redlining, her mind hijacked by memories.

Abdominal pain that brought her to her knees. Blood staining her thighs and dripping onto the cracked tile. The fear on Kurt's face when he found her...

So weak. So helpless.

Goddammit. She didn't have time to get sucked into her past now.

This isn't real. It's part of Rose's plan. It had to be. The alternative... *No.* Whatever was going on, she had to stay ready.

"It's Glenn's," Rose said, through a whimper, her voice weak and thready. "We were…lovers."

Rose's words were like buckshot to the chest. Lovers like hell. Either he'd forced himself on her, or she'd been desperate enough to try to seduce him. Right now, Caitlyn would gladly kill him again.

Christophe sneered and looked her up and down. "He had many."

Rose's face pinched. "I know. But I loved him."

"It's your lucky day, then." Christophe's lips curved into a nasty grin. "You can face his killer."

"*You?*" she asked him, the words thick with disgust as if he were covered in dog shit.

"No, your sister." He stepped back and waved toward Caitlyn.

She would take Rose's look—the trembling O of her mouth, her crumpled brow and accusing brown eyes, the gray cast of her cheeks—to her grave.

"Caitlyn…?" She sounded like a little girl whose illusions about the world had been shattered. "You killed him?" Rose erupted into tears. "How *could* you?"

Christophe laughed and leaned over, getting right in Rose's face. "Nice try, *bouzin*. You could have been an actress. But if you loved Glenn, you wouldn't have tried to run."

With a fierce cry, Rose swung her arm around and plunged the small knife that Caitlyn had slipped to her into the side of Christophe's neck.

Holy shit.

"Aaggh!" He made a strangled sound and grasped at the wound, blood spurting onto Rose, the concrete floor, his clothing.

So much blood. Just like Glenn. Nausea climbed into Caitlyn's throat.

Rose scrambled to her feet and turned away from Christophe as he went limp. Using the roughhewn wooden wall to hold herself steady, she bent at the waist and vomited. She sobbed and heaved and coughed.

"It's okay," Caitlyn said, her own stomach roiling. To her knowledge, Rose had never even held a weapon, let alone hurt anyone. Caitlyn would have given everything to trade places with her in that moment. To spare her sister that act. "You had to."

Rose wiped her mouth on her loose shirt. "I know." Squaring her shoulders on a fortifying breath, she rushed to Kurt's corner as if she hadn't just killed a man and lost her lunch.

She was a goddamned Amazon.

Rose cut his bindings and handed him the knife with trembling hands, sinking to her knees as he freed Caitlyn.

"Are you okay?" Caitlyn asked, rushing to drop to the ground beside her, only several yards from where Christophe lay silent and motionless. She couldn't think about him. Her sister and Kurt were the only ones who mattered now.

Rose scooted back, putting at least a foot of space between her and Caitlyn. "I don't know." She looked up with watery eyes. "I can't regret that." Her shaky hand waved at the dead man. "I couldn't think of another way, but I'm not sure I'll ever be okay with it."

"I understand." More than she wanted. "I'm sorry." Caitlyn pressed the heel of her palm against her thigh. Was there anything she could say to make this better? No. "But you were brilliant."

Rose took a deep, shuddering breath and clasped her hands in her lap. "Did you really kill Glenn?"

The door swung open and the other guard stuck his head in. "What's going—"

Kurt crossed the floor in two strides and punched the man square on the chin. Baldy hit the floor, out cold. With Caitlyn's knife, Kurt cut a piece of rope from the coil that their captors had used to bind them, and secured the man's hands and feet.

He grabbed the AK and nine mil, slinging the rifle over his shoulder, and then approached Christophe, circling around him from behind. He crouched low and felt for a pulse. Catching her eye, he shook his head.

"Let's go." He rose, took the .45 from the dead man's thigh holster, and handed it to Caitlyn.

She made sure it was loaded and the safety was off, and then held out a hand to Rose as she stood. "Our car is just down the road. Do you think you can you make it?"

Rose took her hand and they followed Kurt as he opened the door and then waved them through after he'd determined the coast was clear.

Skirting around the main building, they stuck to the shadows as much as possible, Rose sandwiched between Caitlyn and Kurt. At the beginning of the long, curving driveway, they hid behind a low wall to study the two guards stationed at the entrance to the resort.

"Did you really kill Glenn?" Rose whispered.

"Yes." Caitlyn's stomach clenched. Stupid. Now was not the time for weakness. "He came at me with a knife, so I shot him with his own gun. Long story."

A tear slipped down Rose's cheek, the trail glimmering in the lights positioned at the front gate. "Good," she said, her expression hard as granite. Her hand slipped down to her belly.

Oh, no. *God, no.* "You're actually pregnant?" Caitlyn's mouth tasted like dirt. It hadn't been another lie in Rose's ploy to get free.

"Yes." Rose bit her lip. "From the first week, he…" She looked away.

Damn Glenn to hell. Keeping an eye on the resort behind them for threats, Caitlyn pulled her sister into a hug, something she hadn't done in years. "I'm sorry. I'm so sorry." She backed away and held Rose's shoulders. "We'll get you through this. I will support you no matter what you want to do, no matter what you need.

Rose nodded. "Thank you."

"Let's go," Kurt said softly.

Caitlyn returned her attention to the guards. Both now faced the road, one of them talking into a radio while the other stood at attention.

Moving as quickly as possible in the dim light, Kurt led her and Rose along the path they'd used to enter the resort hours earlier. They approached the Land Rover and piled inside and buckled in, and the car started without incident. Nothing moved in the dark night but the jungle vegetation fluttering in the breeze. Caitlyn's spirits rose. They might just make it after all.

A quarter mile down the street, she rounded a bend and slammed on her brakes. Three large, black SUVs spanned the road from jungle edge to edge, completely blocking her exit. She threw the Land Rover into reverse. A bullet splintered the windshield. She screamed and stomped the gas pedal.

The car lurched backward as she spun the wheel to perform a nausea-inducing about face.

"Go!" Kurt shouted.

She slammed the car into Drive and the wheels spun with a screech before catching purchase. They catapulted forward. Right into the front of a black sedan. A sickening crunch stopped them cold as Rose cried out.

No. They'd been so close. She glanced at Kurt and then at

Rose. "Everyone okay?"

"Yes," Kurt and Rose said in unison.

"What about you?" her sister asked.

"Pissed but uninjured." She was pretty sure. The buzzing in her ears would go away eventually.

Two men stumbled from the sedan and aimed their rifles at the Land Rover. More men rushed the sides of the vehicle and tried to open the doors, but they were locked. The only thing she'd get out of pulling the gun she'd stolen was a bullet in the head.

"Open the doors," one of the guards called through the window, pointing his gun at her head.

"Too bad Brandon didn't spring for the bulletproof glass."

"Yeah," Kurt said, popping the door locks from his side.

Caitlyn watched helplessly as he and Rose were ordered to unlatch their belts and then tugged from the car.

The guard did the same to her, then aimed his weapon at her chest. "You will die for the men you've killed." His quiet voice vibrated with hostility.

Caitlyn's stomach turned to lead. She'd failed Rose. And Kurt.

"Stand down." A familiar voice called as a man strode into view, his icy blue eyes scanning the scene, lit by multiple car headlights.

Caitlyn gasped, body-slammed by the shock.

Glenn Lambert was alive.

CHAPTER FOURTEEN

SHE'D FINALLY LOST HER MIND. Caitlyn blinked several times to clear her vision.

It didn't work.

Glenn still stood in front of her, casually dressed in a linen button-up shirt and chinos, maybe a little pale, a slight hunch to his shoulders, but absolutely not dead.

What. The. Fuck? She'd killed him. She'd even warmed somewhat to her role as executioner.

He gave her a greasy smile. "Rumors of my demise were greatly exaggerated." Cocking his head to one side, he said, "Fortunately, I can't say the same for my father."

Her body turned numb. "You finally did it."

"Not me." He shrugged. "Semantics. It is done. With enough money, you can fake your death and buy someone else's." His grin widened. "It's good to be rich."

Dread did a spider-crawl down her spine. Treavor Lambert had been a criminal in the service of his greed. A professional, despite his despicable business. Glenn was a different kind of evil. Volatile and cruel.

He turned his attention to Rose, who stood next to Kurt, the blood on her shirt a stark contrast against the white fabric. "It seems your sister isn't the only one with a penchant for killing. I hope you both enjoy dying too."

Rose turned sallow, even as she thrust out her chin and pursed her lips defiantly. If Glenn's reappearance was hard for Caitlyn, it had to be infinitely more so for Rose, who'd suffered directly at the man's hands.

Any lingering regret Caitlyn had harbored for killing the man vanished.

She'd never wished to be dreaming more than at this moment. The slimy bastard with expensive loafers and a small army now threatened the two people she cared for most in the world, and there wasn't a goddamned thing she could do about it.

Her stomach clamped down tight. There had to be some way out of this, something she could do to save Rose and Kurt. Something she could do to end Glenn and his awful enterprise.

Caitlyn couldn't let him win. He couldn't fucking win.

Her mind raced. Could she attack the man behind her, start a diversion? If she rammed Glenn, could she take him out before his men shot her? Maybe— *Shit.* Everything she came up with only got her killed without saving anyone.

Think, Cait.

A man with light brown skin and a glistening ponytail marched up to Glenn.

The Lambert heir nodded to Ponytail. "Alvaro, tie their hands. And make sure they're checked *thoroughly* for weapons this time." His gaze flicked toward Caitlyn. "When you're done, bring them to the promontory."

Promontory was too strong a word for the brief rise in land at the tip of the peninsula on which the resort was built. That did nothing to ease the leaden feeling in Kurt's stomach as one of Lambert's guards pushed him, Caitlyn, and Rose through the trees and into a clearing that led to the edge of a sixty-foot cliff.

Glenn had left them stewing for hours—each facing a different wall and forbidden to talk—while he did God knows what, but the light was still too dim to make out the landscape. Kurt could only hear the waves hurling themselves at the rock walls below.

There had to be some way to get them out of this. He'd been a PJ, for God's sake. He wasn't afraid of leaping into the abyss, and he was a top-notch swimmer, with or without his hands bound. They'd fucking practiced that in training.

But even at his peak, he wouldn't have been able to defeat all these armed men with his hands tied behind his back.

Man of Steele, my ass.

Not only would attempting an escape be suicide—he could die with that—but he'd likely get Caitlyn and her sister killed for his efforts.

That he couldn't abide.

Ten yards from the drop-off, Glenn ordered them to stop. He stood before Caitlyn, glowering down his imperious nose at her. "You tried to kill me."

She met his gaze, her chin lifted, glorious in defiance as the stiff breeze stripped her hair from its ponytail and swirled the cloud of dark copper around her head. "In self-defense."

"You took advantage of my father's generosity to try to ruin my family."

"I saved his life. You're the one who murdered him." Her hands clenched behind her back, but she gave no other outward sign of emotion. She was beautiful, incredible. As brave as her old nickname suggested.

Kurt's heart cracked open.

Glenn sneered, his face twisted and cruel in the faint glow of sunrise that filtered through the nearby trees. "He had too many rules. You should have let him die. Then all of this could have been avoided."

"No," she said, deathly calm. "I should have done a better job of *killing you.*"

He slapped her.

Kurt jerked against his captors and growled. The men holding his arms stumbled, but held tight. If he were free, he'd kill Glenn with his bare hands.

Red welts rose on Caitlyn's left cheekbone. The fucker had hit her hard.

Glenn gripped her chin and she flinched. They locked gazes.

Birds chirped. Palm trees rustled. Waves crashed. Men sighed and shifted their weapons. Kurt invented a dozen never-before-imagined ways of killing a man.

"I will make you suffer before you die." Glenn's horrible smile would have given the Devil pause. He released her face with a push and placed his hands on his hips as he faced Kurt and Rose. "Which one do you love more?" he asked, with a grand sweep of his arm in their direction.

Caitlyn tensed and looked at them both in turn.

"That's right." Glenn waved a hand in their direction. "You choose who lives."

Her head whipped back to him, eyes wide. "*What?*"

He gave her an insolent shrug. "You heard me."

Kurt's veins throbbed with urgency.

At Glenn's nod, the guards ushered Kurt and Rose toward the cliff, staging them dangerously close to the edge about twenty feet apart, on either side of a buttress of crumbled boulders that churned the deep blue waters far below. Prodded by rifles, they turned their backs to the ocean to face their executioner.

"No!" Caitlyn fought against the men who held her arms, kicking out at Glenn's legs.

"Enough!" He put his index finger right in her face, a vein in his forehead threatening to pop. "You will choose, or I'll have my men shoot all three of you, right now."

"Four of us."

His pale brows slanted. "Four?"

"Rose is carrying your baby. Baby makes four."

God, the beautiful woman never gave up.

Glenn scoffed and shook his head.

Jack Cartwright cleared his throat and stepped forward. "Actually, sir, she's right."

"*What?*" Glenn's harsh voice lashed the air.

The Hulk's jaw tightened. "When she was at the clinic, the doctor confirmed it."

"That little cock rat could have been with anyone." Glenn gave the large man a dismissive wave and returned his attention to Caitlyn. "Enough of this." He crossed his arms. "Both of them are going over the edge. You are free to follow—and try to save—whomever you choose."

Kurt met Caitlyn's stricken gaze with a small shake of his head. He'd been on borrowed time for six years. If he died now, after he'd finally made love to the woman he'd craved for more than a third of his life, after he'd finally told her what was in his heart, so be it.

But he wouldn't go without a fight, especially if he could improve Caitlyn and Rose's chances for survival.

"At least untie them," Caitlyn said.

Glenn gave her a withering look. "This is not a game. This is vengeance." He leaned in, his face mottled red, eyes nearly slits. "Death by bullet or water?"

Tears tracked down her cheeks and Kurt died a little inside. "Water," she whispered, the tortured sound nearly lost on the wind.

Glenn snapped his fingers and the guards on Kurt and Rose gestured for them to shuffle closer to the edge. Rose cried out, her face wet with tears and snot.

She couldn't swim.

But Kurt could. Like a fucking fish.

Two men held Caitlyn back as she tried to yank free.

Kurt drank in the sight of her as she met his gaze. Auburn hair shimmering in the golden light, the spatter of dark freckles across her beautiful face, those mesmerizing eyes as green as the jungle at her back.

"I love you," he mouthed.

Her lips parted, and she froze. "Kurt—"

He turned and leaped into the sea.

CHAPTER FIFTEEN

"KURT!" CAITLYN'S HEART COLLAPSED AS he disappeared over the edge.

He was a strong swimmer, and the jump was survivable if he went in feet first, but his hands were tied and his legs might weigh him down. Were they buoyant? She had no idea.

To her right, her sister screamed and jumped as the guard moved to push her off the cliff.

"No! *Rose!*" Caitlyn twisted in her captor's grasp.

Glenn jerked his chin and backed away from her. The iron grip on her arms disappeared and she stumbled, caught off guard.

Then she rocketed toward the cliff.

At the last minute, she diverted her path and thrust her shoulder into Glenn's midsection.

He cried out, desperately trying to regain his footing. Instead, he ran out of earth and they both went over the edge. Growling in rage, he grabbed at her face.

Too soon, they crashed into the cool, choppy water and onto the rocks a few feet below the surface. She landed on him, momentarily stunned at the impact as her body bounced and rolled toward the deeper water, sucked away from Glenn and the cliffs by a retreating wave turned pink with blood. Paddling to keep her head above water, she gasped for breath.

Something snagged her ankle, momentarily pulling her under. She fought her way to the surface and looked back. Glenn's hand encircled her lower leg. Blood streamed down the side of his snarling face.

Twenty yards away, Rose's head popped out of the water.

She disappeared again.

"Rose!" Caitlyn used her free leg to kick at Glenn's head until she connected. She pummeled him again and again with her foot until his grip released.

Finally free, she dove for Rose.

If Kurt knew anything, it was how to hold his breath.

As part of his PJ training, he'd spent six weeks in the Special Forces Combat Diver Qualification Course "drown-proofing" himself. Which basically meant learning how to overcome the fear that overtakes a man when he can't breathe.

Occasionally, it meant actually passing out and having to be yanked to the deck where he woke up being slapped in the face, the trainers hurling questions at him. After a quick visit to the medic for some fluids, he'd be back in the pool in under an hour.

He was practically part sea mammal, and if not for his bound hands, and the fact that his legs were half dead weight, he could have been out of rifle range in seconds.

Instead, he dolphin kicked across the sea floor—he only needed a few feet of water to protect him from bullets—fighting to stay below the surface. His prosthetic legs weren't heavy enough to counteract his body's natural buoyancy.

Bright dots swam into his vision, dancing like fireflies on a summer night as his lungs begged for him to breathe.

Crouching, he pushed off, rocketing toward the surface. If he survived, he'd write a glowing letter to the manufacturer of his military-grade legs, which were still functioning despite being submerged in seawater. They had been marketed as waterproof, but this went above and beyond.

He breached the water and gulped air. Gunshots blasted the space around him, pinging into the water near his head. Something hit his leg with a dull, metallic *clang*. So much for being spared death by bullet.

Diving fast, he wedged himself against a ledge halfway down, still safe from the hail of gunfire, but closer to oxygen. Moving quickly, he worked his wrists against the sharp rocks at his back, the waves pushing and prodding to dislodge him from his perch as he tried to ignore the burn in his lungs.

Ow, fuck. He'd caught his right forearm on an edge and a small stream of blood swirled around him. Hopefully, the sharks were busy elsewhere.

He'd nearly reached his limit when the bindings gave way. The rocks slashed his arm again, but he was *free*. Up for more air.

Inhaling sweet oxygen, he pulled hard against the current, his shoulders and arms on fire as circulation was restored. His legs weren't made for swimming, but he got the job done with a sloppy kick, propelling himself toward the far side of the outcropping.

Bullets peppered the water above him as he dove again. His entire body tightened in anticipation of getting hit.

When he broke the surface for another breath, gunfire still echoed across the water.

His thighs burned. He pressed on.

Finally out of sight of the gunmen, he clung to the rocks

for several deep breaths and then worked his way around the pile of boulders toward the other cove below where Rose had been standing just minutes earlier.

A motor sounded nearby. *Shit*. If Lambert's men were on the water—

An ocean swell lifted him enough to see a small boat approaching from the open water, carrying a lone figure with no obvious weapon. The salt water and the sun's reflection off the water blurred his vision. He blinked but couldn't make out who was in the dinghy.

He waved it back. The guards weren't very accurate with their AK-47s, but the boat was well within the rifle's effective range. Too close.

But then he realized the shooting had stopped.

The outboard motor roared as the little boat crested a wave and dropped into the trough.

"Hey!" A trim man with short gray hair and a deep tan kneeled in the boat, wearing only board shorts and sunglasses. He threw out a lifesaver.

Kurt stuck one arm through the ring and awkwardly paddled toward the dinghy. The man helped him up and into the boat.

"There are others," Kurt said, pointing north, his arm heavy as lead. Had they made it? Fear and despair were a rip current threatening to drag him under, but he refused to accept that Caitlyn and Rose hadn't survived.

Already turning, the man said, "My daughter and I saw everything from our boat." His accent marked him as American. "What the hell's going on?"

"We got in the way of a human trafficking operation."

"Shit."

"Pretty much." Kurt surveyed the cliffs. Why had the gunfire stopped? "Thank you for picking me up."

"I tried the police but got no response."

Kurt's heart skipped. "Thank God for that. Most of them are part of it."

"Wish I could say I'm surprised."

As they rounded the last pile of rocks into the next cove, the reason for the sudden silence became clear. On the promontory, Glenn's men were on their knees, hands in the air. Shaylee's friend in the police force must have come through. The other victims would be rescued. Score one for the honest cops.

But right now Kurt had another priority.

As the entire inlet came into view, his blood turned cold. Red water shimmered at the base of the cliff.

And then Caitlyn breached the ocean's surface, swimming toward him on her side, gripping an unconscious Rose across the chest.

"Caitlyn!" He sat up in the boat, energy surging through him. *She's alive.* His throat closed up and he blinked a few times.

The old man tossed Caitlyn the life ring and pulled Rose into the boat, raising an eyebrow at Rose's bound hands before using a knife sheathed at his waist to cut through the ropes. His fatigue forgotten, Kurt ignored the unbearable urge to reach for Caitlyn and moved to deal with Rose as the other man helped her sister climb aboard.

Kurt put his ear next to Rose's nose and mouth. No air. No rise and fall of her chest.

He checked for a pulse. Nothing.

The engine whined and the dinghy made a sharp turn away from shore.

Caitlyn sat at Rose's feet, gripping the handle on the side of the boat. "Is she breathing?"

He shook his head and laid Rose as flat as possible.

Angling as close to her chest as he could get in the confined space, he tilted her head back to open her airway and check for obstructions. Finding none, he pinched her nose shut and gave her two rescue breaths. Then he started chest compressions, trying to find a balance between using the right amount of force and staying low enough that he wouldn't topple into the sea, ignoring the fire in his right arm.

Within seconds, the engine shut down and the little watercraft bumped up against something. Kurt finished his first round of compressions and checked for breath. Still nothing. *Come on.*

"*Rose.*" Caitlyn cried.

"Come here." An unfamiliar woman's voice came from his left, but he didn't stop to look.

Kurt was vaguely aware of the small boat emptying as he fell into a routine, his training taking over as he repeated the CPR cycle. Halfway through his third round of chest compressions Rose vomited, mostly water.

He rolled her to her side and cleared her airway, but she still wasn't breathing. She still had no pulse.

Caitlyn let the twenty-something brunette lead her onto the sailboat only so she wouldn't be in Kurt's way as he worked on Rose. A sob escaped Caitlyn's lips and she dropped onto a bench overlooking the dive platform.

"I'm Tessa Murphy and this is my dad, Oliver," the woman said as she laid a towel over Caitlyn's shoulders. The skin revealed by her bikini top and shorts already betrayed a lifetime of sun exposure. "My dad and I have been moored here for several days. We had just come on deck this morning when we saw you up on the cliffs. He tried to raise the harbor police, but couldn't get through."

"Good," Caitlyn said. "We can't trust them."

Tessa's brow furrowed. "What happ—

Rose vomited and Caitlyn's heart jerked. That was a good sign, right?

But Kurt rolled her onto her side, cleared her airway, checked for breath and pulse, and went back to compressions.

Please, please. *If she lives, I'll be the best damn sister ever. I'll tell her every day that I love her. I'll never push her away again.*

Caitlyn's mind had betrayed her. All those defenses she had built up over the years to protect herself from the hurt and pain of losing someone. First watching Kurt go over the edge, and then Rose. The brick had crumbled and emotions now pierced her walls as easily as arrows through paper.

This was what she'd spent her entire adult life trying to avoid. It hadn't been worth it. Not by a long shot. She'd allowed herself little of the joy, but still suffered all the pain.

And now she might lose Rose. If anyone deserved to be fighting for her life on the floor of that boat, it was Caitlyn. *She* was the one who pushed everyone who mattered away. The one who floated through life without bringing any value or joy to others. The one who hurt those who cared about her most by walking away.

How are you any better than your dad?

The truth gutted her. Just like her father, she had effectively abandoned everyone.

The most important people in her world were both on that dinghy, fighting for her sister's life. They were everything good in this world. Self-sacrificing, honest, compassionate. And for some reason, they both loved her.

Rose threw up more seawater, and this time she started coughing. Coughing meant air.

Oh, thank God. Caitlyn slid to her knees on the deck and forced herself not to rush the dinghy.

Her sister quieted and tried to push herself up. Kurt put a

hand behind Rose's shoulders and helped her sit, murmuring to her. Her wet clothes clung, betraying the slight curve of her belly.

Rose listened and then shook her head.

"Okay," Kurt said, sliding his other arm beneath Rose's knees. "Ready?"

She nodded and he lifted her high enough to hand her off to Oliver, who carried her up the step to the deck and sat her on a bench that ran parallel to the boat's starboard side.

Tessa rushed over with a dry towel and then backed out of the way.

Tears streaming down her face, Caitlyn mouthed "Thank you," to Kurt and scrambled to her sister's side. "Are you okay?"

Stupid question, but Rose produced a weak smile and rubbed a hand over her chest. She'd probably have bruises, but all that mattered was that she was alive.

"I was so worried. I'm sorry, Rose." Caitlyn gave her a gentle hug, careful not to put any weight on her or restrict her breathing in any way.

Rose tapped her throat.

"You can't talk?"

This time she tapped her nose, and Caitlyn laughed, still feeling shaky, but happier than she'd been in years.

"As soon as we get to land, I'll call Shaylee. She's been a wreck."

Tears welled in her sister's eyes and streamed down her sallow face. Caitlyn squeezed Rose's hand and sat down next to her, blinking against the burn in her eyes.

At the aft of the boat, Kurt helped Oliver secure the dinghy, and then they huddled with Tessa, speaking in low tones. Kurt's arm dripped blood. Why wasn't he doing anything about his injury?

The group broke up and the young woman passed Rose and Caitlyn on her way to the cabin, as Oliver started the sailboat's backup engines. "I'll be right back," she said, disappearing into the belowdecks.

Kurt slowly made his way over and stood in front of Rose, putting his hands on his thighs to look her in the eye. "So, I'm Kurt Steele, by the way. I'm a paramedic and a friend of Caitlyn's. How are you feeling?"

Rose reached up and hugged him so hard she almost knocked him off balance. "Thank you," she croaked.

When she released him, Kurt straightened and looked up briefly, blinking. Then he gave her the easy smile that made Caitlyn's heart tilt. "Of course." He cleared his throat. "Uh, hey, we need to get you to a hospital for observation, okay? Probably twenty-four hours just to make sure you don't have any complications. Let me or Caitlyn know if you have increased trouble breathing or any other symptoms that worry you." He glanced at her belly, but didn't say anything about the baby.

"Okay."

"Kurt," Caitlyn said, gesturing to his arm, "you're hurt. Were you shot?"

He glanced down and stared for a second. Then he grimaced. "It's fine. Just a graze from a bullet and some sharp rocks. Tessa went below for the first aid kit." His gaze returned to her. "You doing okay?"

Without thinking, she stood and wrapped her arms around him. "Thank you for saving her."

He gripped her tight. "*You're* the one who dragged her out of the water. Honey, you were goddamned amazing."

She ran her fingers through his wet hair and pressed kisses to his face. "I thought… God, Kurt, I thought you were…" She sobbed and pushed back so he only held her shoulders. "You *jumped*!"

"Hey," he said, his voice hoarse. "So did you." He tucked a piece of damp hair behind her ear and shivered. "I was scared out of my mind—"

She kissed him hard.

Before he could even respond, she pulled out of his embrace and dropped onto the bench, her heart staging an escape attempt.

It was too much. Her body was on emotional overload. She could hardly breathe.

Kurt caressed her hair and then let his hand drop as he turned away, striding to the helm to speak to Oliver. She almost chased after him.

Tessa emerged from the cabin bearing blankets, bottled water, and a red first aid kit. She gave the first two to the women. "We should be ashore soon, but if you need anything else, let me know."

"Thank you," Caitlyn said. "For everything."

Tessa smiled. "Absolutely. I'm just glad we could help."

When the woman left them alone, Rose gripped Caitlyn's hand. "You saved me," Rose said, her voice sounding like it had been sandpapered.

"You doubted?" Caitlyn squeezed her hand and took a deep breath. "I know I suck at this, but...I love you, Shortcake."

Her sister smiled and then coughed, her tight curls dripping water. "I love you too." They watched the turquoise water in silence as the boat sliced through the waves like a jet through the sky.

"I guess I should finally learn to swim," Rose said.

They both laughed, a bit hysterical after everything that had happened.

"God, I missed you," Caitlyn said. "I'm sorry for

abandoning you and the family."

"You're here now. You came for me."

That would have to count. Maybe one of these days Rose and Mike and their mom would forgive her.

Rose's free hand slid low on her abdomen. After a full minute, she said, "I'm going to keep it." Her voice was coming easier now.

What to say to that? The little one was innocent, but could Rose bear to love or keep a child conceived under such circumstances? And while she knew that Shaylee loved her sister, relationships had fallen apart under far less strain.

Rose met her gaze. "I deserve to have something beautiful come out of this."

Caitlyn swallowed hard, her throat tight. Biology didn't matter. She would love Rose's baby as much as she loved its mother. "I'll support you no matter what."

Rose took her hand. "I know." Where did her strength of conviction come from? She trusted Caitlyn more than Caitlyn trusted herself.

Caitlyn's gaze strayed to her left where Kurt now sat on the back bench, covered with a blanket while Oliver wrapped the wound on his arm—finally—and Tessa steered the boat.

Kurt locked eyes with Caitlyn. She ached to go to him, but she wasn't ready to face the enormity of her feelings.

Embracing him and his love meant giving up everything she'd worked for. Not just her business or her dream life on Barbados.

One didn't lightly take a sledgehammer to the last of her defenses.

What if his declaration, his attraction wasn't real? What if it had been the novelty of seeing her again after so long? Or the adrenaline rush that came with the danger they had been in? Or lust mistaken for more?

She didn't trust her own feelings any more than his. How could she, when she had no experience with them?

Love was supposed to be beautiful and wondrous and make you happy. So why was looking at Kurt so painful?

Rose squeezed her hand, pulling away her attention. "He's not like your dad," she said. "Or mine."

A little shock hit Caitlyn's chest, a pebble dropped into smooth water. How did Rose know?

"Dad," Tessa said from behind the helm, her voice tight. "We have company."

Off the port side, several speedboats approached, lights flashing. The St. Isidore Royal Police.

No. Caitlyn's pulse thundered in her ears. They had almost made it to shore. There was nowhere to run.

She locked eyes with Kurt, reading the same concern that strummed her veins. If these cops worked for the Lamberts, everyone on the sailboat was dead.

CHAPTER SIXTEEN

THE POLICE OFFICERS WHO PICKED them up were the good guys. Which didn't mean Kurt and the others were home free immediately. It took three days of hospital visits, police interrogations, and legal negotiations. He was ready to sleep for a week.

The prosecutor decided not to press charges against any of them. Finding the new batch of trafficking victims had helped. As had several of Lambert's men cutting deals to start talking.

Shaylee's organization—STOP—and the police were working together to identify and locate the remaining victims IPI had placed in homes and businesses across the Caribbean.

Kurt had the impression that the government wanted to deal with the police corruption and human trafficking as quietly as possible, and that putting Americans on trial for killing two of those involved—Glenn did not survive the injuries he sustained in the fall from the cliff—would only put more of a damper on the much-needed tourism industry.

Other than the Lamberts, everyone's names had been

kept out of the news.

Tessa and Oliver Murphy were allowed to resume their summer-long cruise of the islands. Kurt had thanked them again and exchanged contact information with the pair, promising to keep in touch.

By eleven on Thursday morning, Kurt, Caitlyn, and Rose were finally free, riding in Shaylee's little car toward Caitlyn's house.

"You think they're truly done with us?" Rose asked. "After everything...it seems too easy."

"Yes," Shaylee said. "It's done. You have the paperwork to prove it."

"Right," Rose said, her hand glued to Shaylee's thigh. "It's going to take a while for that to sink in though."

She had recovered from her near drowning, and the baby did not appear to be adversely affected by the trauma, though only time would tell. Shaylee was sticking by her side, and had assured them that she'd encourage Rose to get counseling to deal with everything she'd been through.

Kurt wanted that with Caitlyn, who sat huddled under the protection of his arm, but not nearly as close as he'd like. He couldn't stop touching her, reassuring himself that she was here with him and safe.

The last few days—during those nights when he hardly slept—had confirmed for him that he didn't need a family, the whole thing that his sister and his friends had, all the trappings of a traditional life.

He would welcome marriage and children. Happily.

But he *needed* only Caitlyn.

And he wasn't sure he could have her.

Clenching his free hand, he focused his attention on the view out the window, on this gorgeous island he would never be able to bring himself to visit again if Caitlyn let him walk out of her life again. They'd hardly had a moment to talk since the police intercepted the Murphys' boat, and he had no idea what she was thinking.

Minutes later, they stopped in front of her house and everyone exited the car.

Rose hugged her sister. "I'll call you tomorrow."

Cait let her go, only to be enveloped in Shaylee's arms, her expression slightly confused but content.

Rose turned her attention to Kurt. "Thank you again."

"Of course. I'm glad you're okay."

She grabbed him around the neck and held tight. "Give her time," she whispered as she stepped back.

All he could do was nod. He'd already given her fourteen years. How much more time did she need?

Shaylee gave him a quick hug and thanks, and then the couple left him and Caitlyn standing on the sidewalk as they drove away.

"You're back!" A petite woman with coal-black skin and graying hair pulled into a bun rushed down the steps of the red house next door, Rockley shooting out the open door past the woman as if on fire.

Caitlyn laughed and fawned over the adorable mutt, hugging him tight and apologizing for leaving him for so long. "Thank you, Jade. I owe you."

"Bah." The woman gave a dismissive wave and smiled. "He's a joy. And you are safe. All's good."

Caitlyn introduced her to Kurt and they made small talk for a few minutes before Jade made her excuses and left so they could go inside.

The minute they crossed the threshold, Caitlyn's shoulders relaxed and she sighed, a deep smile on her face. "God, it's good to be home."

Rockley circled her, his tail whipping her knees as he

nudged her hand. "I missed you too, buddy." She crouched down to rub his face and neck. "You're a good boy," she murmured.

She belonged here with her dog, in this colorful little house, on this island, far away from the unpredictable weather and crowds and craziness of DC.

And he didn't. His family, his friends, and his business were in Virginia.

Could he really ask her to give up this—her dream life—for him?

Leaving Caitlyn and Rockley to catch up, he gathered his toiletries and stuffed the clothes he'd unpacked into his carry-on. He didn't need to leave for the airport for another three hours, but what else did he have to do?

The faint scuff of a shoe on wood alerted him to Caitlyn's presence, but he didn't turn.

Her palms caressed his upper back, warm through the thin cotton of his T-shirt, and slid down and around his waist as she embraced him. She laid her head between his shoulder blades and he stilled, covering her hands with his own. "Thank you," she said so softly he almost couldn't hear.

"For what?" His voice was rusty and battered as a tin can left outside for years.

"For everything. For not turning me away when I showed up at your office, for putting yourself in harm's way to help me. For saving me and Rose. For everything except jumping early. I will never thank you for that." She sucked in a shaky breath and pressed her forehead against his spine.

Dammit. He turned in her arms and pulled her into his embrace, stroking her hair and kissing her brow, unable to stop himself from touching her now that she was here, smelling so fresh and sweet and crying over him.

"You're the one who stopped Glenn and saved your sister

from drowning," he said. His chest tightened at how close they'd all come to dying. "I'm just so goddamned glad you survived."

"I'd kill that bastard again in a heartbeat."

Kurt cupped her face and caught her gaze. "Are you really doing okay with it?"

She focused on his mouth. "I'm fine. No regrets."

"Really? If you ever need to talk…" Old argument. She already knew his offer was open.

Her eyes were green as a forest and softened when she smiled. "Truly. But if that changes, I promise I'll find someone to talk to."

Someone. He wanted it to be him, but better someone than no one.

"Honestly," her palms slid under the hem of his shirt and up his back, "right now, talking is the last thing I'm in the mood for."

Heat slithered through his veins. If she couldn't love him, he should walk away. But he'd never been that strong. Not when it came to this woman.

"Are you sure you can't stay?" she asked.

His pulse tripped. "For how long?"

Her expression faltered. "I…I don't know. You're the most incredible man I've ever known, and I love being with you. But I'm broken, Kurt. I'm not sure I can ever surrender myself to a relationship the way you deserve." She stroked his brow. "I don't want to lead you on, give you hope that I can change."

His heart became a hard knot in his chest. "Get some help and I'll wait for you to be ready. You're worth it to me."

She looked away. "That's not… I can't ask you to do that."

Can't or won't? Maybe they were the same thing.

A few days ago he might have been tempted to take whatever she had to offer, but she was right. He deserved more than half a relationship. He wanted her all in—as invested as he was—or not at all.

And he needed to honor her wishes and quit pushing. Clearly her feelings weren't on the same level as his. He loved her enough to respect her choice and let go.

It might be the right decision, but it still sucked ass.

"Then this is goodbye," he said, his voice tight.

Tears shone in her eyes, and she gave him a sad imitation of a flirty smile. "You have three more hours. How do you feel about an extended sendoff?" It was the vulnerability in her voice, the uncertainty in her gorgeous green eyes that did him in. In this moment, she wanted him as much he wanted her.

He wasn't fool enough to say no.

She raised her face and their lips met. Instant bonfire. A lightning strike. *More*. He wanted more of her taste and the soft rasp of her tongue and the scratch of her fingernails across his shoulders. She reached for the hem of his shirt and he released her so she could pull it free, pausing to make sure she didn't catch the bandage on his forearm.

Her fingers drifted over his chest and abs reverently. "You're amazing. You give new meaning to the word chiseled."

Pride puffed his chest and her touch sent sparks across his skin. "I'm probably overcompensating."

She laughed. "I doubt that. You must drive the girls at the gym out of their mind."

He shook his head. "It's not that kind of place." The other workout junkies were mostly disabled veterans like himself. It was a safe space where they could let down their guard and work on improving their bodies without being ogled by the curious. But he didn't want to talk about other women or the gym.

He tugged on her shirt and she shucked it and her bra before he even had a chance. He groaned at the sight and covered her breasts with his hands, kneading their soft weight. "You are so beautiful. I want to kiss every single freckle on your body from head to toe."

Her brow wrinkled. "You do?"

"Yes, please. Starting with this one." He leaned in and touched the tip of his tongue to the tiny spot on the edge of her upper lip, then he gently sucked.

She moaned and leaned in, opening to his kiss. Her hands slid inside his waistband as she moved to unbutton his pants. She got them undone, and he grabbed her hands before she could push them over his hips. His heart jackhammered in his chest, but her gaze was soft and open.

"I don't care about your scars," she said. "What I care about most is up here." She gently tapped his forehead. "The rest is window dressing."

What she cared about, not loved. But she *did* care. That mattered. He swallowed hard and dropped his hands.

"Have you been totally naked with anyone since...?"

Unable to speak, he shook his head. If there was ever going to be a person he trusted enough, it was Caitlyn. And even though he couldn't keep her, he would kick himself for the rest of his life if he didn't take what she offered him now.

Slowly, she pushed his pants to the floor, leaving his boxers in place. Then, she removed her shorts and panties and stood nude before him, maybe somehow understanding that this was easier if he wasn't the only one in the room who was vulnerable.

His bag landed on the floor with a thud as he pushed it aside and sat on the bed. Taking off his prosthetic legs wasn't strictly necessary, but they wouldn't exactly be soft and cuddly against her skin.

Without looking at her, he released the suction on one socket and removed his right leg, and then repeated with the other one. With his latest flexible socket and carbon-fiber frame, he no longer used liners or socks on his stumps, so he simply rubbed his limbs for few seconds and sat back to look up at her.

She'd seen him like this before, but now she went to her knees before him and his cock jumped at the sight of her naked and kneeling with her luscious lips so close to his lap. "Is there any pain?" she asked. "Can I touch you?"

God, yes. Anytime. "You won't hurt me."

With shaky fingers, she rubbed her hands over his thighs, around the puckered scars at the blunt ends of his residual limbs, and along his hard-earned quadriceps muscles, through the dark leg hair and up under the edges of his boxers. He could easily succumb to the temptation to close his eyes and lie back, but he stayed seated, mesmerized by the view.

He only had a few more hours with her. He didn't want to miss a second.

Caitlyn's cool fingers on his skin were heavenly. His breath came faster, and she carefully tugged on the front of his underwear, prodding him to lift his hips so she could remove it. And then her hands were covering his erection, stroking firmly and driving him out of his mind.

Reaching down, he pulled her on top of him and lay back, kissing her mouth, her chin, her neck, nibbling at her shoulders and licking his way down her chest until he suckled her nipples, alternating between the sweet pink buds until she arched and gave a low moan. He wanted more. More skin on skin, more heat and friction. More...everything.

Rolling, he trapped her beneath him. Her eyes fluttered

open and she smiled. He kissed her, exploring her mouth, running his hand down the smooth skin of her stomach and into the slick heat between her thighs. She raised her hips and he found the core of her pleasure, stroking until she gasped and shuddered and called out.

"Kurt, *now*."

He shifted his position and slid home.

Moving slowly, he sank deeper with every thrust, giving her body time to adjust. She bucked up against him, taking all of him. He lost control, driving into her as she gripped his buttocks, urging him on.

Sweat rolled down his back, tickling the base of his spine where the tension built. He balanced on his arms, consumed with the addictive sensation of Caitlyn under him, clenching around him. His breath stopped. His chest coiled and then burst apart in a shower of light and sparks behind his eyes as the energy inside him filled the room.

He was in free-fall, as if hurled from a plane, both weightless and plummeting. Pure rush.

"I love you, Caitlyn," he said on a gasp, sucking air and collapsing to his elbows, trapping her beneath him as if he could hold her this way forever. "I love you."

Caitlyn could have stayed cocooned in Kurt's embrace for an eternity. How this strong, intelligent, breathtaking man of integrity could love her, she would never fathom.

Nor could she fully articulate why she couldn't give him the words back. She hadn't lied about being broken. More like defective. What if her watered-down version of love wasn't enough for him? What if she never learned to give fully of herself? A man like Kurt was entitled to so much more than a second-rate lover. He deserved a chance to find the kind of happiness another woman—a normal woman—could give him.

A better woman than her.

She fought against the sting of tears and kissed him softly, sweetly, and thoroughly, hoarding memories of his taste, the rough slide of his tongue, his masculine scent.

He raised himself onto his elbows and she traced the outline of his tattoo.

He smoothed the hair from her forehead, pressing his lips lightly to her brow as he eased from her body, leaving her empty and aching.

They stared at one another, her heart fluttering in distress at his expression. His espresso eyes lacked their usual bright intensity. His brows, the muscles at the outer corners of his eyes, his mouth, all pulled down as if too heavy for him to muster even a hint of a smile.

Without a word, he rolled off her, slid to the floor, took a few things from his bag, and walked on his stumps through the bedroom door and into the bathroom.

This wasn't how she wanted their time together to end, but no matter how many times they made love, eventually they'd have to say goodbye. Caitlyn rolled to her stomach and pressed her face into the bedspread that was now marked with his scent.

Panic rampaged through her veins. How could she give him up?

How could she not?

They spent the next two hours avoiding topics of any gravity, eating lunch, and playing with Rockley before Caitlyn drove Kurt to the airport.

Their parting was far less enthusiastic or demonstrative than his arrival. Ironic given that they were supposedly faking their attraction back then, and now he was half of her soul.

He gave her a far-too-quick kiss on the lips and brushed

his thumb across her cheekbone. "Take care of yourself, Braveheart."

Then he was gone, lost in the crowd of tourists before she could formulate a response.

CHAPTER SEVENTEEN

AT FIVE O'CLOCK ON A Friday in early December, Kurt ended a conference call with a new client's COO and sat back in his squeaky chair. Outside his office window, the lights of the monuments came alive as the sky turned dark.

Six weeks ago, he'd walked away from the never-ending summer of Barbados and the woman he loved. It already felt like an eternity. Unfortunately, he couldn't remove the part of his heart that ached for her.

Work mostly kept his mind busy during the day, but at night… He worked himself half to death in the pool and the weight room just so he could sleep.

Running a hand through his hair, he sighed. Like with any healing, this would take time. At least that's what his sister kept telling him. He should know better than anyone.

On the plus side, he was no longer afraid of flying. Small comfort.

Tara tapped lightly on his door, interrupting his maudlin musings. "Hey," she said, leaning in from the hall.

"You taking off?"

"Yeah, but there's a woman here who wants to talk to you about a bodyguard. Do you have a few minutes before you leave?"

"Sure." They didn't get many walk-in clients, but it happened on occasion. "I'll close up."

"Okay, thanks."

"Have a good weekend," he said, rising from his chair to follow her to the lobby.

"You too." She flashed him a huge smile and rushed down the hallway with her overstuffed blue purse on her arm. Maybe she had big plans for once.

By the time he reached the reception area, the heavy front door was already hissing closed behind her, the automatic, after-hours lock clicking into place. Plastering a benign smile on his face, he rounded the Christmas tree Tara had placed next to the couch for the upcoming holiday.

And stopped breathing.

Caitlyn sat in the center of the long sofa, knees together, hands clasped in her lap. She wore a puffy blue parka and a green scarf that matched her eyes, her silky hair tucked under a knit hat.

He almost laughed. It wasn't *that* cold yet.

"Hi," she said, wiping her palms on her jeans as she stood.

His heart lodged in his throat. "What are you doing here?" he asked, his words harsher than intended.

She bit her lip and nodded to herself, as if she'd expected an angry reception. "Rose and Shaylee decided to move to the States—to Boston—so they could get married before the baby comes. Barbados doesn't allow same-sex marriage, and Shaylee found a job with a human trafficking prevention organization in Somerville. It's fucking cold, but they seem happy."

He stared, drinking her in, still not entirely sure if she was really here talking a mile a minute, or he was hallucinating. But Tara had seen her, right?

"Anyway, I decided to follow them," she said.

He couldn't stop watching her mouth, tracking that little freckle as her lips moved. "To Boston?"

"Oh, um, no. To the States." She took a deep breath and blew it out. "To here, actually. Northern Virginia."

"Why?" Was he thick in the head? Because she couldn't possibly be hinting at what he hoped. "What about Barbados and its perfect weather, and your little house, and your charter business?" Her sunshine scent curled through him, warming his blood like a fine whisky. Holy shit, she was really here. "And your dog?"

She laughed. "It was time for a change. I left the beautiful weather—which I may already be regretting—" she rubbed her arms and gave an exaggerated shiver "—and the house and the tourists behind, but I brought Rockley and my plane with me. I can run short-haul flights anywhere."

He could only stare.

"God, I suck at this," she said on a sigh. She shook her head and inched around the coffee table until she was only an arm's length away, close enough for him to see the streaks of gold in her eyes. "Because I missed you. Because even though I'm terrified I won't be enough for you, or that you'll realize I'm not worth the trouble and walk out on me, even though you could *hurt* me like no one else, I desperately want to be with you."

That made two of them, but he didn't move. None of those were the words he needed. "You didn't want to call first? Maybe let me in on your plans?" Really, her expectation that he was just moping around waiting for her like some lovesick loser irked him. No matter that it was true. "Not a word from you for six weeks, and now you show up out of the blue and I'm supposed to…what? Let you walk back into my life and trample all over my heart again? I thought we were done, Caitlyn. What if I've moved on?"

Pink splotches appeared on her cheeks and she chewed on her lower lip. "Have you?" she asked in a hoarse, quiet voice.

Damn her. He crossed his arms and broke eye contact. "No."

"Kurt," she said, regaining his attention. She licked her lips and looked up at him through her lashes. "I'm sorry. I wanted this to be a grand gesture. To show you how serious I am." She dropped her arms to her sides, elbows locked straight with her hands balled into fists. Her chin lifted and she looked him dead on, emerald eyes shining. "*Goddammit*, I love you."

A low buzzing filled his ears and his chest floated, but… *Caution*. "How do you know? What's changed?"

"Nothing. And everything." She lifted her hands and dropped them, huffing out a breath. "I think maybe I've always loved you, but I needed time to make sure it was real. To know that I could trust my feelings and fully commit. I was goddamned miserable after you left, but even after I realized what a fool I'd been to let you go, it took me a few more weeks to stop being a coward about it."

"You've never been a coward."

She scoffed. "I'm scared out of my freaking mind. Maybe I always will be. My dad left me. My stepdad left me. Aaron…" Her hand waved away the man's name as if she couldn't bear to have the word in the air around her.

Kurt couldn't blame her.

"I'm afraid you'll leave me too," she said, wounding him. "Not because I don't trust you—you're the most honorable man I've ever met—but because there's a part of me that will probably always believe that no relationship with a man can be trusted. That men don't stick around. Not with me, anyway."

His stomach knotted.

"I've finally found the courage to put myself in your hands, to take a chance that you won't 'trample all over my heart' either. I know you deserve better than an emotionally damaged woman who can't give you a family, who is skeptical of marriage and happily ever after. But I'm hoping, maybe, you love me enough to overlook all that."

She had given up everything to come here and lay herself bare to him. He understood how big a deal that was.

"Can we…" She swallowed hard and took a step closer, holding her arms across her ribs. "Can we try again?"

"Because you love me?" he asked, his voice gravelly, his stomach fluttering.

"Yes." Her eyebrows lifted and her lips curled into the barest hint of a smile. "I love you."

He could hardly breathe. "You might have to tell me a few more times before it sinks in."

Her smile grew. "I will tell you every day for the rest of my life. I love you, I love you, I love you."

He'd never be able to hear it enough, but that would do for now. Unable to suppress a grin, he closed the gap between them, hauling her into his arms. She wrapped her legs around his waist, almost knocking him off balance, and he kissed her, his whole body sighing as he sank into her lush mouth, drunk on her fresh-air scent and cinnamon taste.

In seconds, he had her pinned to the wall, holding her up with one arm as his other hand roamed. First order of business: jettison the damned parka. He unzipped the monstrosity, pulled it off her arms, and then slid his hand under her fuzzy sweater, seeking the softness of her breast.

She moaned and attacked his mouth with her own, rolling her pelvis against him. With a little push, she freed her legs and stood, tugging off her scarf and cap with a crackle of static. Strands of her hair stood up straight, floating around her head in a halo. "I should have worn a dress."

"God, yes." He kissed his way down her neck. "Always wear dresses." She was beautiful in anything—and he knew for a fact she wasn't a dress fan—but he was fully on board for easy access.

Unwilling to take his hands and mouth off her, Kurt didn't make it easy, but with a minute of fumbling, she managed to free one of her legs from her jeans and push his khakis and boxers down to his hips. Far enough.

Impatient, he lifted her again, shoving aside her panties, and then he was inside of her and it was…everything. *She* was everything.

Trapped against the wall, Caitlyn clung to him, offering little breathy moans as she kissed his neck and dug her fingers into his shoulders. Her body grasped him tightly, creating an electrifying friction as he thrust and withdrew, drawing out the pleasure until he couldn't bear it. He pistoned his hips, giving all of himself and his love to Caitlyn, every part of him pulling up tight, balancing on the edge of a precipice.

"I love you, Kurt." Her breath brushed his ear.

His orgasm rocketed through him. He had just enough awareness to reach between them and bring her along for the ride.

Stars fell around them as he kissed her eyes and cheeks and mouth over and over. *Never enough.*

Caitlyn laughed and leaned her head against the wall. "Hang on, Superstud. I need to catch my breath."

His legs were locked, but his limbs trembled as his body

cooled. Pushing off the wall, he gripped his pants as he stumbled to the couch and sat, her heat still surrounding him in the most delicious way.

"One of these days we'll go slowly enough for me to kiss you everywhere," he said, letting his head drop against the couch cushions, even as he kept a tight grip on her hips.

Her sexy smile made his dick jump with renewed interest. "Ditto."

Actually, everything about her made him want to spend the next week in bed, exploring her from head to toe, cataloguing every curve, every scar, every freckle. *Thoroughly.*

She ran her fingers through his hair and he closed his eyes. *So good.*

"While I have your attention," she said, "I have a favor to ask."

"Anything." He opened his eyes and got lost in her emerald gaze. He could never refuse her.

"Rockley and I need a place to stay. Do you know anyone with a room for rent who doesn't mind dogs?"

Was she serious? "I have a spare half a bed. Or is that too much too soon?"

She smiled. "*No.* I just didn't want to pressure you…or assume anything."

"I'd rather not waste another day. Fourteen years is long enough to wait before moving in together, don't you think?"

"Definitely." She toyed with his shirt collar, her face turning sober. "As long as it won't bother you that I squeeze the toothpaste tube from the top."

"Trying to warn me off already?" If she was this scared, maybe she really did love him.

Her mouth twisted and she shrugged.

"I'm not that petty, but if it worries you, buy your own damn toothpaste. We don't have to share *everything*." He nipped at her sweet mouth. "Winters are cold here, you know."

"I noticed."

He chuckled. "This is nothing. Wait until February."

She gave a resigned sigh. "Well, you said you run hot. I'm sure you can figure out a way to keep me warm."

He sucked on her soft, warm bottom lip. "I already have a hundred ideas."

She caressed his cheeks and frowned.

"What?" he asked, gently tugging on a strand of auburn silk that fell across her face.

"You know I can't have kids. And I'm not sure I'll ever want them, adopted or otherwise." A little crease formed between her brows. "Someday you might resent me for that."

Finally, her real concern. He grasped her hands and kissed her fingers. "I'd love to raise children with you, and even get married if I can ever convince you to take that leap of faith. But I wasn't lying, Cait. None of that matters without you. At the very least, we'll have Rose and Shaylee's baby and Luke to spoil rotten. I'm content to be an uncle."

A tear slipped down her cheek and she swiped it away. "Truly?"

His heart swelled, too big for his chest. "Truly." He meant it, but he'd probably have to convince her daily. Lots of fun ways to accomplish the task came to mind. "Besides, we have fur kids."

She bit her lip and nodded. "I hope they get along."

"They'll learn." He smoothed his hands over her staticky hair. "What do you say?" He dug his keys out of his pocket. "With this house key, I thee cohabit?"

She laughed and then studied him for a long moment, as if measuring the truth in his eyes. "Yes." A thousand-watt smile lit her face and she kissed him hard. "Yes, and I love you."

He couldn't hold back a satisfied grin. Or stop touching her. "That's all I need to know."

AUTHOR'S NOTE

The waterproof, microprocessor knee that Kurt uses is real. If you'd like to see it in action, check out https://www.ottobockus.com/prosthetics/lower-limb-prosthetics/solution-overview/x3-prosthetic-leg/.

With advances in materials technology, today's amputees also have new options for sockets. The prosthetist I met with is a fan of using a soft socket that's supported by a rigid carbon-fiber frame, rather than the completely rigid socket that most people are familiar with (check out this page for photos: https://www.amputee-coalition.org/resources/options-in-sockets-and-liners/). The flexible socket allows some amputees—like Kurt—to wear their prosthetic limb without any kind of liner or sock, and can be more comfortable, especially when sitting. Or when being sat upon. ;-)

Unfortunately, as Kurt told Caitlyn, not everyone has access to the latest in prosthetic technology. While amputee service members and veterans from post-9/11 armed conflicts are offered multiple prosthetics for various activities, state-of-the-art microprocessor joints, and frequent replacements, this is not the experience for some older veterans and most civilians.

For more behind-the-scenes info and fun facts about this book, check out the *Running Blind* page on my website.

THANK YOU!

Thank you for reading *Running Blind*. I hope you enjoyed it!

Sign up for my **newsletter** at gwenhernandez.com/newsletter to learn about new releases, and be entered for a chance to win my next book.

I'd love to hear from you! Feel free to contact me at one of the sites below.

Website: gwenhernandez.com

Twitter: @Gwen_Hernandez

Facebook: www.facebook.com/GwenHernandezAuthor

Goodreads: www.goodreads.com/gwenhernandez

Reviews help readers find books. I'd sincerely appreciate it if you took a minute to leave a review for *Running Blind* on your favorite retailer or book review site.

If you missed Dan and Alyssa's adventure on St. Isidore, keep reading for a sneak peek from *Blind Ambition*.

Thanks!

MEN OF STEELE

Blind Fury

Blind Ambition

Blindsided

Running Blind

BLIND AMBITION EXCERPT

"Packed with action and emotion. BLIND AMBITION is a page-turner!" --*New York Times* bestselling author Laura Griffin

IT'S ABOUT TO GET HOT IN THE JUNGLE

Rescuing a kidnapped aid worker from St. Isidore's dangerous rebels is just another day at work for former pararescueman Dan Molina. But his mission falls apart when the woman—who once shattered his heart—refuses to leave the island.

Alexa Alyssandratos can't return to her life as a nurse on the hurricane-ravaged Caribbean island, but she won't leave until she's certain the orphans she cared for—especially one sick little girl—are safe from the rebels. Denied their ransom, a would-be dictator and his soldiers are hunting Alexa, and Dan is the only person who can protect her. Old passions reignite as she and Dan race to save the children before they disappear forever.

CHAPTER ONE

Alexa lowered the trembling girl into the crawl space beneath the clinic and shut the trap door. She yanked the braided rag rug to cover it and stood. Soldiers would be here any—

The exam room door smashed open and a rangy man in a striped rugby shirt aimed a rifle at her chest. "Hands up!"

Heart hammering, she stepped onto the rug and raised her arms.

The last time the island's rebel fighters had raided the Hygiea clinic in Terre Verte, they'd stolen everything—right down to the mattresses on the beds—and left one of the nurses dead. The mother of nine-year-old Flore. Flore, who should be safe at the orphanage next door by now.

As long as the stress—and the dust under the building— didn't bring on another asthma attack.

"Just tell me what you need and I'll get it for you," Alexa said, her voice shaky.

Rugby kept his weapon trained on her. "Come with me."

Her stomach jackknifed, but she followed him into the tiny waiting area where two other men stood guard.

He snagged her wrist and spun her into the front wall. "Do not fight me and you will live." His lilting island tones didn't match the menace in his voice.

A tremor ran through her body as he trapped her against the wall. Just last month a French aid worker in another village had been kidnapped and repeatedly raped until her family produced a ransom. Would they take Alexa because she was American?

The man drew her hands together behind her, sending her into panic mode. She knew how much rape could devastate a person. She'd witnessed it firsthand with her sister. No way would she go down easy. Not as long as she had any fight left. Alexa kicked back, connecting with her attacker's shin and eliciting an enraged howl.

"*Bouzin!*" he yelled, calling her a bitch. He knocked her feet out from under her and she slammed to the ground, hitting her cheekbone and hip on the solid wood before he landed on her.

She bit back a whimper and flailed like a madwoman. All of

the self-defense moves she'd learned were useless now that she was down.

"No more moving." Rugby ended her fight with a knee to her back and shackles around her wrists and ankles.

Shouts came from the storage room that doubled as her sleeping quarters. She turned her head to see Garfield in the doorway, a rifle trained on him from behind. His lip was split and bleeding, and his dark eyes blazed with anger when he spotted her.

Hands out, palms up, he stepped forward. "Why do you fight us? We'll let you take whatever you need. We'll treat your men. No need for violence."

Rugby stood. "You'll let us take her." He kicked Alexa in the ribs and she hissed in pain.

"Stop!" Garfield lunged toward her.

A soldier in a yellow shirt jumped forward and plunged his knife to the hilt in Garfield's side, then pulled away. Blood ran through her friend's fingers as he gripped the wound and sank to his knees, his eyes wide.

"Garfield!" Alexa jerked against her restraints. "*Let me help him.*" Her voice turned shrill as Rugby gripped her under the arms and tossed her over his shoulder, setting off a firestorm of pain in her ribs that left her gasping.

Her captor strode to the door, pausing to call directions to his crew, who appeared in the doorway of the back room with their arms full of medicine, blankets, and syringes.

Then he stepped outside into the moist Caribbean air, and Alexa watched through the doorway—absolutely powerless— as Garfield's blood drained from his body, sliding into the cracks between planks in the scuffed wooden floor.

* * *

Want more? Get BLIND AMBITION *in e-book or paperback at your favorite online retailer.*

ABOUT THE AUTHOR

Growing up, Gwen Hernandez wasn't brave enough to share the stories in her head with other kids, but they usually involved intrigue and romance. She was raised in the Army and Navy, and married an Air Force engineer, so it's natural that her Men of Steele series features military heroes and heroines who must overcome danger to find true love.

In her off time, she likes to travel, read, jog, flail on a yoga mat, and explore southern California, where she currently lives with her husband and a lazy golden retriever.

Made in the USA
San Bernardino, CA
11 January 2018